W9-BTD-130

After Annie

After Annie

A NOVEL

MICHAEL TUCKER

OVERLOOK
NEW YORK, NY

This edition first published in hardcover the United States in 2012 by
The Overlook Press, Peter Mayer Publishers, Inc.

141 Wooster Street
New York, NY 10012
www.overlookpress.com
For bulk and special sales, please contact sales@overlookny.com

Cataloging-in-Publication Data is available from the Library of Congress

Book design and typeformatting by Bernard Schleifer
Manufactured in the United States of America

2 4 6 8 10 9 7 5 3 1

ISBN 978-1-59020-735-2

I dedicate this book to a girl I picked up at a party while my wife was talking to somebody in the other room. That was forty-two years ago and I still can't get her out of my mind. Sometimes a woman hooks you and you know the hook is set so deep it's never coming out. This book is for you, baby.

All men should strive to learn before they die what they are running from, and to, and why.
—JAMES THURBER

CHAPTER ONE

H ERBIE AARON CAN'T BELIEVE HE CAN'T FIND A BAR. HE pulls his cap down, turtles his head into his coat and works his way south on Madison Avenue, crossing Ninety-sixth Street. "In the middle of New York fucking City," he mutters and a gust of wind fairly blows him through the window of the Rite Aid. A few snowflakes swirl around his head. It's too cold to snow, he tells them. Herbie passes a faux-French bistro, which has shut down for the night. Deep inside his coat, he shakes his head with disdain. It's not until he's into the Eighties that he finds a bar with the lights on, an upscale place just off the avenue, down a couple of steps, with its name written in blue neon script on the window.

"A boite," he says. He pushes the glass door, which makes a satisfying whoosh and he's out of the howling cold into the cushioned murmur of the bar. "A fucking boite."

Herbie talks to himself. He thinks these conversations all take place inside his head but he's wrong about that. He'll talk, he'll work things out—like what he's going to say when he gets to a party—over and over, making little adjustments until he's happy with it. Sometimes he'll argue with people, or lecture them—and even if he manages to not move his lips, you look at his face and it's obvious there's a whole three-act play going on in there. There was a woman in the Fairway, talking on her cell phone with her shopping cart parked sideways in the middle of the aisle, hundreds of gourmands in both directions unable to move, unable to shop. Walking back to his apartment he lit into her—with gestures—all the way up West End Avenue. He went on about her arrogance, her narcissism. She tried to argue back but he skillfully parried any attempt at self-justification. He verbally pinned her to the board like a butterfly, deftly, disdainfully. Don't fuck with Herbie.

He checks out the long bar and heads to the loneliest spot at the far end and piles his coat and hat on the stool next to him. Down at the other end are two couples who seem to know each other and one old guy alone, well dressed, staring into space.

"I'm an old guy, too," Herbie says, maybe out loud, maybe to himself; he can't tell anymore.

The bartender is all the way down at the other end, pouring white wine from a magnum. He can't help but notice she's a knockout. He cleans his glasses with a cocktail napkin just to make sure. She finally deigns to notice him and she gives him a look about how far she's got to walk to get to him.

"Last call," she says.

He holds his hands out, palms up—is there no justice?

Her extraordinary mouth twists up in a smile. Lots of dark hair, pulled back off her face, cheekbones to die for. "Some of us have been here since five this afternoon," she says.

"I missed happy hour."

She nods. "You probably want a drink."

"Vodka rocks—a double. And if this is really the last call why don't you bring me four of them?"

"Oh great, a drunk. I'll bring you one. Then if you're a good boy, I'll bring you another. Belvedere? Grey Goose?"

"You have something in a cheap American vodka?" He gets a laugh as she walks away.

It wasn't his glasses. She's the real thing. He watches appreciatively as she pours the double and walks it back to him.

"Why you looking at me like that?" she asks as she puts down his drink.

"You're the second-best-looking girl I've seen all day."

"Your wife the first?" she says, gesturing to his ring.

He nods and smiles. She returns the smile and a smudge of red shows up on her cheek. Girls love it when you love your wife, he thinks.

"So what are you giving that look to the first girl that brings you a drink?" She's an East Coast girl by the sound of it. Maybe Connecticut.

"If I could stop looking I would."

He watches her walk back down to the other end to close out the customers. "If I had a granddaughter," he says philosophically, "she would be older than this girl." He takes a deep sip of the vodka and feels it go down. No amount of booze is going to make a difference tonight. *"You are too beautiful, my dear, to be true,"* Johnny Hartman is singing on the jukebox. Jukebox? It's a *sound system*, asshole. Nobody calls it a jukebox. He snorts at himself and takes another deep pull. *"And I am a fool for beauty,"* sings Johnny.

Booze is a woman, some guy told him once. Like having another woman on the side. That's why it always makes his wife so crazy. A guru told him that, one in a long line of gurus he and Annie played with in the old days. Oh, they did some shit in the old days. They were a caution. They crossed the line and crossed it back again. It wasn't the booze so much that drove her crazy. It was more when he drank and smoked reefer at the same time. She really hated that. She said he changed—that his personality changed. Which wasn't true at all, according to him. "I'm inside here, where you can get a very good look at the personality," he says. "And believe me, it's the same." Once, in a seminar they took up in Northern California—a weekend course at a hippie hot springs kind of place about some Hindu sex practice—they ended up getting it on with a couple of girls who were there on staff as sacred priestesses. The four of them got a room and rolled around for hours, trying all the combinations. "Girls," he says to the ice in the bottom of his glass, "are great."

The other couples and the old guy pay up and say good night and the gorgeous bartender brings him another double.

"This one's on me," she says. "Then you gotta go home."

"You're tired, I know." Herbie half drains the glass and then gives her his sad, wise empathetic look—a look that he has down cold. She edges closer to the bar.

"Are you famous? Those people were saying you look like that actor."

"Which actor?"

"I don't know. On television."

"Think about it: if you have to ask, how famous could I be?" Then he shoots her his wry, soulful, self-effacing look. This look almost won him an Emmy. She moves, if possible, even closer to the bar.

"So, where's your wife?"

"Sleeping."

"Lucky her."

He finishes the drink and slides the glass across like he's putting her in check. She gives a half smile, half sigh and goes and pours him another. When she brings the drink back, she mimics his slide move.

"So who are you?" she says.

"What do you do when you're not buying drinks for people?"

"I sing. I'm a singer." And again, the red smudge shows up on her cheek and Herbie thinks that if she could patent that blush, she could own the world. He makes a picture—a little club down in the Village, smoky, funky; she's on a stool with the single spotlight framing her face; sad love songs, yearning songs; every guy in the room wants to make her feel better.

"A chanteuse."

"Yeah, I guess. You like heavy metal?"

Ping! Fantasy shattered. Herbie lifts his eyebrows and nods to her, like he's saying "Hey, that's great! Love that stuff!" She laughs out loud and walks away.

"Sure, Herb," he says to himself—when he talks to himself, it's Herb. "She sings sad songs in the Village in a smoky room—on the jukebox."

The lights go on and Herbie flinches like he's been hit with a stick. There is no more depressing sight in the world, he thinks, than when the work lights come up in a bar. Everything you came for disappears—including the next drink. He drains the watered-down booze at the bottom of his glass. He could have used the fourth one. He leaves her ample money and wrestles himself into his coat and hat. "Heavy metal, my ass," he says as he whooshes back out into the empty night.

The tenth floor at Mt. Sinai has lighting as bad as when the bartender turned the lights on. Everybody looks like they're in a porn film. Herbie waves to the night nurse and she calls him over.

"She's still sleeping, Mr. Aaron."

"Good. I'll be quiet." The nurse gives him a nice smile and he gives it back to her. Annie's room is dimly lit, just a small lamp next to the armchair at the foot of her bed. He clears some things off of it—some books and a *New Yorker* that he'd brought over earlier—and settles in. She looks to him like she's eight years old, snoozing away without a care in the world. He wishes he knew her then.

Three months ago they were trodding the boards, as they say. They were doing a musical together—Off-Off-Broadway, where the salaries are dazzling. They had a ball, working with young people, dancing and singing. All the kids idolized them like they were the Lunts or something. We're the Lumps, he told them, a lesser-known show biz couple. One night they came offstage after a scene in the second act and he whispered to her as he always does, "How'd you feel?" The next scene was already playing so they quietly picked their way past the stored scenery pieces and props on their way to the dressing room.

"Good," she whispered back to him. "Better tonight, I thought."

"Yeah, me, too. I finally got the laugh on that fucking birthday line. Only took me seven weeks to figure it out." They were now in the hallway.

"You mean when you say, 'It's not my birthday'?"

"Yeah. A big laugh—finally. I played it like I couldn't believe you thought it was my birthday after all these years and . . . what?"

She was smiling and shaking her head.

"What?"

"That was me, honey."

"What was you?"

"When you turned away, I did this little thing with my eyebrow—like this."

She showed him how she raised her left eyebrow in an expression of "give me strength."

"Brought the house down," she said with barely concealed smugness.

"You were making a face on my line?"

"Oh come on, it's not your line. It's our line. When one person is talking, the other one doesn't go dead. It's a scene between two living people." He stops at the water cooler to get a drink.

"I thought I had finally figured out that moment."

"Nope."

They had met in their early twenties—thirty-eight years ago at a repertory theater in Cleveland. They were both in the cast of a production of *Mother Courage*. He was married to someone else and she was fresh out of drama school. They couldn't keep their hands off each other. He courted her with Samuel Beckett, quoting lines from *Waiting for Godot*—all about how we're all trying to fill up the time so that we don't have to think about how meaningless and desperate our lives are. It may not sound like much of a come-on but he knew his girl. By the second week of rehearsal they were sneaking off to her apartment for a quickie whenever the director was rehearsing a scene they weren't in. They'd drift back singly so that no one suspected they'd been together, but the leading lady, an old movie star from the days when European divas were all the rage, had them figured out from the get-go. *"Somebody's been fucking,"* she'd sing out, sniffing the air, when either of them walked into the green room. Getting caught was almost as much fun as the sex.

Herbie closes his eyes and lets his chins drop onto his chest. He has a few different scenarios for getting to sleep. Either he thinks about all the different girls he's had sex with—any kind of sex—starting with the first breast he ever touched and the girl who was attached to it—Judy Fritchen, who, at thirteen, had an intricate set of rules about what could be played with and what couldn't. Or he goes through various sports moments that he had when he was still limber—the key moments, like a highlight reel. Or—his favorite fantasy—he thinks back to when he was a spy in the Second World War, working with the French Resistance. He had been trained to kill with his bare hands in a matter of seconds. He received this training when he was working with the British commandos and the Free French in England. His fluency in French and German was why they first approached him—and his background as an actor, of course. They trained him to master every conceivable weapon. He not only became a crack marksman, but he learned to take the various guns apart and reassemble them in a pitch-dark room. He learned hand-to-hand combat, knife techniques, parachuting, scuba. He could blow bridges. He had been dropped into Brittany and hidden by partisans in a farmhouse until he was ready to make his way into Paris with a new identity and passport—that of an automobile parts salesman from Dijon. The farmer's daughter, a radiant, natural, piquant beauty, came every night to his straw bed, hidden in the barn, but she was still a bit too young; there are rules about these things. Perhaps after Paris, after he'd assassinated the Gestapo chief and stole the top-secret files, she'd be just old enough.

His snoring wakes her. Annie's eyes blink open and she sees him slumped in the chair with his head at a horrible angle and his mouth wide open. He could wake the dead, she thinks, and she smiles. He would like that joke. The pain drip makes everything an effort—to see, to hear, to talk, to breathe. But she shakes her leg out from under the covers and pokes him with her toe. No answer. So she pokes him harder until he stirs. He looks around for a moment and when he remembers where he is, he lets out a big sigh.

"Yeah. This fucking place," Annie says. He nods and rubs his eyes.

"Where was that hotel?" he asks, still half dreaming. "Outside Saint-Tropez—where I had to sleep in the bathtub?"

"Ramatuelle. That hotel was good, actually. I slept really well."

"I was passing a kidney stone."

"Yeah, but the hotel was nice."

He reaches out to hold her hand. "Why'd you wake up?"

"You snored."

"Fuck me," he shrugs. "Like life."

"Just like life."

"You need your little sound machine. I'll bring it."

Herbie pulls the chair over. Annie gestures him onto the bed. They hold hands for a while.

"How's the drugs? Need more?"

She shakes her head.

"I'll take a hit if it's going around," he says.

"Did you go to a bar?"

He nods and grunts.

"Did you get drunk?"

"No," he says. "Can't."

"You're going to have a headache. Take some aspirin."

"You worried about my health?" He kicks his shoes off and crawls in beside her, careful not to disturb the drip. "Try to sleep some more."

"No," she says. "I like this." They shift around to get comfortable.

"Put your leg where I like it." He does. They know this position. They've carved it in the stone.

"Are you going to be mad at me when I go?" she asks.

"You're going?"

"Yeah."

"Fuck that."

They lie there in quiet for a long time, chewing it over.

"We leave each other all the time," he says. "We leave each other a thousand times a day."

"Yeah; different."

They think about all the times they've left each other. Herbie starts to rub his thigh between her legs.

"You leave every time after we make love," she says. "You go away."

"You hate that."

"I'm used to it."

"That's actually different."

"Oh yeah?"

"It's more like a meditation. It's the only time I'm truly calm. I go into a kind of alpha state."

"You're snoring away like a lumberjack. Meditation my ass."

They start to laugh softly together. This is too good, he thinks. I'll never have this again.

"There was a gorgeous girl at the bar. The bartender."

"Tell me."

This is an old game with them. It used to be like foreplay but these days it's more like nostalgia.

"Her face was the deal. She had a very provocative mouth."

"Mmm. You like a good mouth."

"I do."

He kisses her softly on the lips; she makes a small sound in her throat—not quite a moan—and they settle into each other.

"Provocative how?"

"It turns down, you know? Like she's been sad for centuries. But a very appealing mouth, very . . . approachable."

"Kissable."

He grunts and kisses her again.

"Like Jeanne Moreau," she offers.

"Yeah, like that, but . . . you remember that girl in the Piero della Francesca?"

"The pregnant Madonna?"

"Yeah. Could be the same girl."

"Wow."

"I couldn't tell about the rest of her. The room was dark and she was behind the bar, but I think she had all the parts."

"Did she want you?"

"Yeah, she wanted me to get out of there as soon as possible."

"You wait, honey. They're going to be lined up around the block. You're going to get all the girls you ever dreamed of."

"I'll put in a revolving door to handle the traffic."

"You'll see."

Herbie didn't want any girls. It wouldn't be any fun without Annie. She likes girls almost as much as he does. In the old days when they would take on a lover together, Herbie would be like the lifeguard—he'd just lie back and watch as the girls got themselves all warm and rosy and then, when the moment was right, he'd allow them to take advantage of him. He'd just be there for whenever they needed what he had that they didn't. Well, sometimes he would take a more active role, suggesting they do this or that, but that usually broke the spell. The girls didn't go for him being bossy. But if he could control himself and just wait until they got the idea, he could have himself some high-class sex.

It's been a while, though, since they have had a lover together. It got too complicated. You never realize how difficult something is until you stop doing it. A third person in your bed can be a lot of fun, but she's a person—with problems and history, with neuroses and habits, with friends and relatives—and believe me, a girl who'll jump into bed with a married couple can have some pretty interesting friends. And finally, every single one of them wanted Herbie and Annie to be their parents, which was the last thing they needed or wanted. So after the last one graduated—they really thought of it that way—they took a break and realized how much easier it was just the two of them. Of course, easier can lead to boring, so every now and then, when the situation presented itself, they would help themselves to a little snack—not a full meal, just an *amuse-bouche*.

"Tell me more about the bartender," said Annie and she ran her finger over his heart, where she knew he was hurting.

CHAPTER TWO

CANDY AARON STRIDES DOWN THE HOSPITAL CORRIDOR dressed to the nines in cashmere and Italian leather, carrying a coffee cake in a little box tied up with string. All the nurses stare in appreciation as she walks by even though they've seen her every morning this week. Candy's got that thing. She's not beautiful, not in the current sense of perfectly regular, cookie-cutter features—but she's a knockout. She has her father's nose—the family honker—which would be a serious detriment on any other face, but on Candy's, somehow, it's an asset. It's like the prow of a ship, a figurehead forging its way through the raging ocean. Whereas with Herbie, the very same nose looks like a big thumbs-down gesture plastered onto the middle of his face. Herbie's nose reminds us that we're not perfect whereas Candy's trumpets our singularity. And then, of course, there's her hair, her astonishing mop—Irish red all tangled up around her face and down around her shoulders. It's like her head is on fire. Candy's hair is her pride, her signature.

She peeks into the room and sees her mom and dad curled up together in the hospital bed like two puppies in a box. She intakes an involuntary, inaudible gasp and tears spring to her eyes. She shakes her head as if to make it go away. Her mom and dad have always inhabited a world unto themselves. When she was a little girl, it was like they were surrounded by a protective circle, a magic bubble that she could never penetrate. Annie and Herb, Herbie and Ann—and then there was Candy. Not that she wasn't wanted and adored, and supported and encouraged. She was their kid, after all. But she always knew that she would never be loved by anyone the way they loved each other. She grew up with that, wearing it like a badge, until it virtually defined her.

She stands in the doorway, one hip cocked expectantly and the string of the bakery box dangling between her thumb and forefinger. She sighs as if her disapproval could wake them. Herbie gets the message and stirs. He waves to her and holds a finger up to his lips. Don't wake your mom.

She gestures, "Should I come back?" Herbie shakes his head.

"I brought coffee cake," she whispers.

Herbie carefully extricates himself from the tubes and takes the cake from Candy, kissing her softly on the cheek. "Thanks, honey."

"God, Daddy, you look like shit."

He nods. "You look good."

Candy raises her eyes to the ceiling and sighs—like the compliment is too much to bear. "Maurice is leaving me."

"What?"

"Yeah. He's seeing somebody else. It's over."

Herbie is not ready for this information. He's slept maybe an hour, tops; he's still half in the bag from the vodka and his words pop out edgy and hostile. "What are you *talking* about?" His voice rises and his head tilts forward on his neck like he's on the attack. "What the fuck are you *talking* about?" All of Candy's danger signals go off—bells, whistles, sirens—and she feels a huge rush of adrenaline. All she can think to do is to attack back. She jabs her finger down into Herbie's face—she's taller than he is, even without the Italian boots—and hisses, "What? What's your problem?"

"This is not the time or the place for your drama," spits out Herbie as if he's talking to a thirteen-year-old. "This is not your time." Candy feels like she's been hit. Her attack mode vanishes and she's suddenly the bruised and bleeding victim. Her chest caves in; she becomes strangely shorter and smaller; her eyebrows are innocent question marks perched above her nose, now the nose of her forefathers, the nose of bondage, persecution and injustice. She shakes her head in disbelief.

"I don't believe you said that, Daddy. That is the meanest thing you ever said to me. What's your point? That I don't care about Mommy? That I don't love her? Is that what you're trying to say?"

"Honey, go home and take a shower." This is Annie from the bed. Her voice is calm. She's the only one in the family who's not stressed out by her dying. Whatever adjustment she's had to make, she's made. Herbie's still all puffed up and he starts pacing the room and sighing.

"Just go, honey. I want to spend some time with Candy. Take a shower and get some sleep. And I'll see you later."

Herbie nods and starts to put his coat on. He looks at Candy a little sheepishly and then tries to give her a kiss on the cheek. She's having none of it. He shrugs and waves good-bye.

Annie pats the bed and Candy sits next to her. They take hands and sit in silence for a while. Annie, who can barely lift her arm anymore, feels stronger than she's ever felt in her life. She has no conflicts, no doubts. She's dying, which feels exactly like the thing she should be doing right now. But—there's always a but—before she breathes her last, she's going to fix everybody one last time.

"Give Daddy a little space, honey. He's lost."

"Fuck him, he's lost. What about me? I'm lost, too."

"Tell me what happened with Maurice."

Candy snorts ruefully, opens the box and breaks off a nice hunk of the cake. She offers the box to Annie, who takes a smaller piece. They get crumbs on the blanket, like they did when she was a kid.

"You remember Susan Hoff? She was Jean-Luc's editor for a while in Paris?"

Jean-Luc is Candy's former beau. He's a documentary film-maker of note—world-renowned, actually. Although Herbie always said he could never figure out how those documentary guys earn a living. Nobody ever goes to see their movies, he says. They just get prizes. But he's one of the best, apparently, and Candy was with him for six years. Jean-Luc is one of those wiry guys that do all the extreme sports—helicopter skiing, trekking in Nepal, double triathlons. And for work, he goes all over the world filming pygmy head-shrinking rituals and things like that. All of which is amazing, given that Candy is a dedicated indoors-woman and always was. But she co-produced four films with him and they were a good team. They had a great apartment in Paris and Annie and Herb got to visit them a lot and they usually had a good time together. Herbie thought a lot of Jean-Luc. He thought he was a very nice guy for a Frenchman.

"Which one was Susan Hoff? I'm trying to picture her. Did we ever have dinner with her?"

"No. She's a Brit. Remember we went shopping, the three of us? At that arcade in the Second Arrondissement? And you bought that green umbrella?"

"Kind of short with big breasts?"

Candy nods.

"I still have that umbrella," says Annie. Candy can see the green umbrella; she knows exactly where it is—hanging in her parents' bedroom closet, on a hook just inside the door. She thinks that she'll take the green umbrella back to her apartment and keep it forever. She tries not to think about it—about what life will be like after Annie is gone—but like a canker sore, she can't stop picking at it. Annie reads her face and punches her softly on the arm.

"C'mon, tell me about Susan Hoff."

Candy composes herself and lets out a big breath. "She's fucking Maurice."

Annie looks at her like she's crazy. "Maurice loves you, honey. I know this. I know the man very well."

"If they're not fucking, they will be."

"How did Susan Hoff get together with Maurice? Isn't she in Paris? Or London?"

"No, she's here."

"And . . ."

Candy puckers up her lips like a little kid and her eyes look up to the ceiling, as if to say, don't look at me, I'm just a little innocent girl.

"Oh, honey. Why do you do this?" Candy has a history of fixing up her boyfriends with women who are perfect for them. She has a 100 percent success rate. Jean-Luc is now married to one of Candy's college roommates and has two kids. They all ski.

"Susan Hoff is a sheep. She's a reasonably intelligent, reasonably attractive sheep with big tits. She's exactly what Maurice needs. He doesn't want a woman; he wants a sheep. And I'm not a sheep.

"What are you?"

Candy sighs and shakes her head. "I don't know—a rare bird, like a snowy egret. I mean I could be a sheep. I've done it before—with Jean-Luc—I was totally a sheep with Jean-Luc.

And a Sherpa. And I was definitely a sheep with Eric Katz. Remember that motherfucker? And I was a sheep with that other guy, the one from Florida. So I could do it with Maurice. I've done it. I mean the clothes are great. And the travel. And Maurice is no dummy, he's brilliant at pretending I have my own life, my own career. He gave me a title, with an office and a secretary, but it's all bullshit. I'm there for him—to be on his arm, to bounce all his brilliant ideas off of, to be in his bed. But finally it's all for him."

"And what's for you? What do you want?"

"I don't know. I told you, I'm an egret—what do egrets know? Sometimes I want to be taken care of and sometimes I want to be my rare bird self."

"What about both? You could have both." Candy sighs and looks long at Annie, who has always had both.

"Easy for you to say," says Candy. They smile and take hands.

"That's your father's favorite joke."

"Which?"

"The guy comes home and tells his wife that the doctor just told him he has ten hours to live. The wife is all upset and says that she'll cook him his favorite dinner—roast chicken with mashed potatoes—and he says no, he wants to make love to her—all night—over and over again. That's easy for you to say, says the wife. You don't have to get up in the morning."

"That's terrible!" screams Candy. But she can't stop herself from laughing. "How come I never heard that?" They laugh together and then they hold each other.

Herbie decides to walk home through the park. He's still pissed at Candy and he wants to walk it off. He also has a new coat and he wants to see if it works in the cold. It's like a regular coat, as opposed to those Michelin Man things that make him feel like he's twelve years old. This is a wool coat—stylish, three-quarter length with nice, deep pockets—and then inside, that you can zip in and out, is a lining made of that Michelin Man stuff, but the thin version—that just keeps you warm but doesn't make you look like an igloo. It's a nice coat. He pulls down the earmuffs that are part of his tweedy little cap and he's all set.

It's the only way she can deal with this, he says out loud with gestures as he crosses into the park above Ninety-sixth Street. She's got to make it her drama. No way Maurice has another woman. Maurice, whatever else he is, is not a fucker. They've lived together four years now for Christ's sake. They do everything together. He proposes to her once a week and she, of course, keeps turning him down. Like all the other guys. Can't pull the fucking trigger.

Oh God, he says, what a thought—Candy on her own again. Please God in heaven. She'll start another one of her careers. Frescoing. Or neuroscience. She'll go back to school—in Bologna or Prague or Helsinki—and I'll have to pay for everything, because, for all her worldliness and experience, Candy doesn't have two dimes to rub together. She's like her mother—no fucking use for money at all. Except to give it away. Please God, she's just being hysterical and they're fine.

Herbie would miss Maurice. The two of them have developed a very nice relationship over the years. He always thought it was considerate of Candy to get together with a guy who was his own age. He and Maurice are four months apart and they get along well. It's also not bad having a friend who gets invited to the Owner's Box at Yankee Stadium. Maurice is a major mover and shaker. He has companies, he's on boards, he gives to the big charities, he dines on occasion with the mayor.

Maurice is one of the great high-level hustlers of all time—real estate, cable companies, some kind of hedge fund, lots of fingers in lots of pots. They couldn't be less alike, the two of them—Maurice being mainstream and Herbie being a boho—but they understand each other in a basic way. Yeah, he would miss Maurice.

There's no way she would lose him, he says. They live in a four-story townhouse down in the Village; they've got the house in Southampton; they've got that cute little jet plane to fly around in. Come on, no way. She should break down and marry him. Which she'll never do because it's not fucking dramatic enough. If she doesn't have a Greek play going on around her, it's not worth her getting out of bed in the morning. It's hard to out-dramatize your mother dying of cancer, but believe me, Candy'll give it a shot.

He starts to rant at Annie, too. How could he? How could he be angry with his wonderful Annie? His life partner, his muse, his heart? Because she's fucking dying, that's why, he yells to the trees. We made a deal—I go first. We signed it; we had it notarized. It was an ironclad deal and she's welshing on it.

It happened so fast he still can't catch his breath. A month ago she was fine. They had her cancer from twenty years ago always hanging over their heads like a scimitar. But they were used to that. And then—in one week—the three words you never want to hear, one right after the other. Recurrence. Metastasis. Riddled.

Despite the earmuffs, Herbie can't get warm. His teeth are rattling like he has a fever. He must have walked two miles easy at this point, ranting and raving and waving his arms, and he's exhausted. Whatever was left of the vodka buzz is gone and he has a full-blown hangover. He turns the corner at Eighty-third Street onto Broadway, right where that big delicatessen is, and there's this guy standing out front, staring at him. The closer Herbie gets, the more the guy is locking eyes with him. Now, this has happened many times—Herbie used to be on TV and people still occasionally recognize him. Or more likely, the guy thinks he knows him but he doesn't know from where. They went to high school together or camp in the Adirondacks. This happens all the time to him. Herbie slows down when he gets to the guy and he gives him the old "how ya doin'" self-effacing smile and the guy holds out a little brown bag to him.

"You like Jewish food?"

"What?"

"I have a half of a bagel-and-nova sandwich. I haven't touched it and I don't want it. Please, take it." He jiggles the bag a little.

"No, I got food at home. Thanks." And the guy looks at him with a really pathetic look and jiggles the bag again and Herbie realizes that the guy thinks he's a homeless person. At the same moment, the penny drops for the guy—like maybe this guy's *not* a homeless person and I just made a big mistake. They back away from each other and start walking in opposite directions—even though Herbie is actually headed downtown, too. Then he stops and thinks what the fuck, and he calls to the guy, "You're really not gonna eat it?" And the guy wheels around and heads back, "No, I was gonna throw it out, I swear."

"You got a little slice of onion on it?"

"Absolutely."

"And you didn't take a bite out of it?" The guy crosses his heart with is free hand.

"What the fuck," he says, this time out loud to the guy, who smiles and gives him the bag, still not sure that Herbie's not a homeless person. They wave to each other and Herbie crosses the street—he's got to get away from this guy.

"What pisses me off," he says out loud, "is the coat. A new fucking coat that cost eight hundred dollars and he thinks I'm sleeping in it. What the fuck is *that* all about?"

CHAPTER THREE

THE NEXT NIGHT, THE BAR IS A LOT MORE CROWDED. Must be a weekend or something, he thinks, as he pushes through the door. The day has been brutal. Some close friends came to visit the hospital and one after another, they fell apart like five-dollar umbrellas. So, of course it was up to Annie to make everybody feel better—which she did in great style. But once they were gone she crashed like a kite. She doesn't have much left.

Herbie heads to where he sat the night before. He sets himself up in the last seat against the wall with three empty stools to the other side. If he could get away with it, he would put his coat over his head. He perches and watches his bartender earn her money, working the crowd, humping drinks like a pro. She never looks his way—he's watching carefully—but then out of nowhere, a double vodka rocks gets plopped down in front of him.

"Hang around awhile," she says. "I have something to tell you." And she's gone before he can answer, off to make fifty more cosmopolitans.

"I'll hang, I'll hang," he says and he kills half the drink in a swallow. The vodka feels good tonight, hitting all the right spots.

If anything, she's better-looking than last night, he thinks. Maybe it's the hustle and bustle but she seems rosier, lit up like the business end of a joint. Herbie sits and appreciates her, mostly getting the view of her back, which is also not a bad thing.

Thank God, he says to himself, I'm old enough to know that I don't want to fuck her. That takes all the pressure off. She's too young, anyway. *Way* too young. There's a cutoff. I mean, please. And young girls, frankly, are not so great in bed. They're always showing how good they do stuff. When you show, you don't feel. Young girls are years away from knowing that. I don't have to have sex with her—I can just appreciate her and take in all her energy and catch a whiff of her. She's gorgeous and she brings me booze; why would I need anything else?

But if by some rare occurrence, he argues, some arcane, oddball thing—like she gets this tropical disease that can only be cured by having sex with an old, sagging, Jewish alcoholic— would he? To save her life?

He's smiling now. He polishes off the drink with another prodigious gulp and puts the glass down on the bar with just enough sound to let her know he's dry. He shakes his head and starts laughing—inside to himself, but plenty is showing on his face.

Who the fuck do you think you're talking to, Herb? Who are you trying to bullshit? Given half a chance, you'd be on this girl like a Yorkie in heat. Given the slightest hint of encouragement, the tiniest crack of an opening and you'd be on your knees, begging. Who do you think you're talking to here, Mary fucking Poppins?

Later, after the bar has cleared some, he sits and waits for her to come his way. She's been keeping his glass topped up. Tonight the vodka works. He's fairly numb.

"I know who you are," she says when there's finally some space.

No you don't, he thinks.

"I googled you. And your wife, too—God, she's so amazing. I didn't realize you two were married. And you're right; she's way more beautiful than me."

Herbie nods.

"What's it like working with your wife?"

Oh Jesus Christ, he thinks. If one more person asks me that stupid fucking question, I'm going to run screaming into the night.

"She wants to meet you," he tells her.

"What?"

"I was telling her about you last night."

"You were?" She can't make her face hide the fact that she's pleased.

"Yeah. I told her I met a girl in a bar who has a face from an Italian painting and I flirted with her."

That red smudge again on her cheek. "What'd she say?"

"That she wants to meet you."

"Really?"

"Yeah."

"She gonna beat me up?"

That makes Herbie smile, "I don't think so. She asked me to tell her what you looked like, so I did."

She stares at him with question marks in her eyes. "What'd you say?"

"That you're very young."

She holds up a finger and rushes down to the other end of the bar, where it's getting busy again. It must be Saturday fucking night, thinks Herbie. He watches her play catch-up, closing some people out, refilling others. He suddenly doesn't feel like drinking anymore. Maybe he's hungry. He has no idea what he is. He waves to her and makes the international gesture for menu and after a while she brings him one.

"I'll bet I'm not as young as you think I am."

"Oh yeah? How not young are you?"

"Thirty-four."

This surprises him. "So there's virtually no chance that I could be your grandfather."

She smiles. "No, I can actually give you irrefutable proof that you are neither one of my grandfathers."

"What's your name?"

She shrugs. "Olive."

"Olive," he says, as if he's about to eat her. "Olive, I would like a cheeseburger, medium rare with fries." He takes a breath and lets it out. "And then I have another, slightly strange request." He holds up his hands in a defensive posture and makes a face like "Don't think I'm too weird."

"Oh God." Her cheeks dimple up a little. "Like you want to me dress up in a costume and say mean things to you?"

"What's strange about that? No, Annie, my wife, asked me to ask you if you would come by to meet her. After you're done with work."

"Why doesn't she . . . ?" Then she stops and cocks her head to the side.

"Is she up at Mount Sinai?"

He nods and stares her down. Smart girl, he thinks. She's got it all figured out.

"Is she gonna be okay?"

He thinks for a moment about whether to get into this with her. Finally, he indicates that no, she's not going to be okay. The girl's face looks like she just got smacked hard. She's stuck for what to say. Herbie reaches across and squeezes her arm. He wants to make it okay for her.

She starts to tear up. "She was amazing."

"She still is."

The girl nods, contritely. "She wants to see me at the hospital?"

He nods.

"Sure," she says, very unsure.

"And never mind about the cheeseburger. I don't know what I was thinking." He pulls out some money and puts it down on the bar. "I'll leave your name at the desk downstairs. We're in 1032."

An hour later, he and Annie are hard into a game of Scrabble on her bed—the travel version that doesn't spill the letters all over the place. Annie is kicking the crap out of him as always. He's behind by forty points and he's desperately trying to find a way to use all his letters so that he can get the big bonus. After a long wait, he lays down a word and turns the board around so she can see it.

"What's that?"

"Pobbledy," he says, nonchalantly.

"As in what?"

"As in, 'That is without a doubt the most pobbledy thing I ever heard.'"

"I don't think so."

"Be very careful—if you challenge and I'm right—*pobbledy*, by the way, is strewn through Samuel Johnson; he used it all the time—then you blow your lead."

"Challenge."

"Think carefully before you act."

Annie glances over Herbie's shoulder, toward the door and smiles. "Hi, Olive," she says. "Come on in."

She came, thinks Herbie. Good for her. In this light he can see that Olive is indeed not a child. There's a sharpness in her eye, an alertness for what might be coming at her, like a boxer moving in. But he also thinks she's one of those girls who's only going to get more beautiful.

"Herbie was just leaving," says Annie, holding her hand out for him. He takes it and kisses her softly on the lips.

Okay, he thinks, Herbie is leaving again. I get it—I'm no fun to have around—I'm chronically morose, I need a shower, I cheat at Scrabble—get this fucking guy out of here. It's good, he thinks, the girl's going to give Annie a better night than I could at this point. They have no history. There will be no regret on Olive's face for the Annie that used to be. On his way to the door he touches Olive's arm.

"So what, you listen to every drunk that comes into your bar with a crazy proposition?"

She laughs.

"Let her get some sleep."

"I will. I'll just sit here; we'll be fine."

As he gets his coat on, he feels that charge in the air that girls have when they get the guys out of the way—probably the same charge they felt when they were nine years old and doing a sleepover. He feels completely excluded, as he always does in this situation. More than excluded; rather like he's a different species altogether, without any of the same DNA—like a cat trying to understand a horse—"Hey man, why do you let them get on your *back* like that?" He doesn't feel any jealousy, which is strange for him. Maybe he's dead, he thinks; that might explain it.

On his way out he asks the night nurse to check the pain drip. She comes in and ups the flow a little and asks Annie if she wants her bed refreshed and Olive says that she'll do it. She slips right into nurse mode, re-doing the bed around her so that it's all smooth and wrinkle-free. She gets some fresh water into Annie's glass and turns the lights down. She's taken care of people before.

"You want to change your nightgown?"

"No, I'm fine."

They take each other in. Annie senses people, so she just sits there for a moment.

"Thanks for coming," she says finally.

Olive nods. She, too, is feeling a charge between them. "Can I ask you a question?"

"Sure."

"Why did you want to meet me?"

"Pretty strange, huh?

"I guess."

Annie's eyes fill with tears. "I'm worried about my husband. About Herbie."

Olive waits.

"So I had to meet the girl who got him breathing again."

"Oh."

"I'm terribly afraid . . ." The tears now release down her cheeks. "One of us has to survive this."

"No, he's . . . he's still breathing."

Annie leans back into her newly plumped up pillows and crosses her hands over her tummy. Her eyes are clouded by the morphine. "So, heavy metal, huh?"

Olive smiles. "No, I've never sung heavy metal. I just said that to your husband because he thought he was being so cool. I wanted to see the look on his face."

Annie gets a kick out of this. "So he was feeling a little frisky, huh?"

Olive blushes.

"What do you sing, Olive?"

"I trained classically—you know, for the opera. But now I'm mostly thinking about musical comedy. I've done some shows— summer stock, stuff like that."

"Would you sing for me?"

"Sure. Sometime."

"I don't have some time."

"I can't sing here. I don't have . . . I mean, we have to be quiet, don't we?"

Annie shrugs.

"How about . . . I have my last singing lesson on my iPod. Do you want to hear that?"

She digs into her backpack for the iPod and puts the earphones on herself. "Let me adjust the volume for you." She listens. "This is the warm-up; you definitely don't want to hear that."

Then she puts the earphones gently on Annie's ears.

In a whisper, "'O Mio Babbino Caro'—Puccini."

Annie closes her eyes and listens, a tired smile on her face. Then she removes the earphones and looks at her for a long moment.

"What happened, Olive?"

Olive tenses.

"You're thirty-four?"

"Yes."

"And you work in a bar?"

"It's my uncle's bar. He's kind of helping me out."

"Tick tock, Olive."

They look at each other.

"Tell me," says Annie. Her voice is tired.

"What?"

"Tell me the story of the exquisite singer who's tending her uncle's bar. I need to hear your story."

"I didn't . . . I don't want to talk about me."

"Sure you do." Annie smiles at her.

"You should rest. I'll just sit here."

"Come on, sweetheart, don't make me pull it out of you. I don't have time."

"I don't know what you want me to say."

Annie appraises her for a long moment.

"Shall I tell you what I see in your face?"

A shiver shoots up Olive's spine. She looks into Annie's eyes, which are suddenly clear and blue. "Okay," she says.

"You give yourself up. To everybody. And you've been doing it for such a long time, you don't know any other way to be."

"Give myself up?"

"You sell yourself out; you take the short end. Again and again and again. And you're so angry about it, sweetheart, it's choking you."

"You don't know me. You can't say that."

"Oh, I know you. I know you like I know my own skin."

Herbie decides to sleep on the couch, the bedroom being too depressing. The whole apartment is an alien, hostile place. He puts a pinch of marijuana into his hash pipe, lights it and takes the whole little bowlful into his lungs and holds it there. That's all he needs—Herbie, the one-hit wonder. He exhales, lays his head on the pillow and tries all his tricks—the old girl-friends, the French Resistance—forget it, not tonight. He's never been more tired and he's never been further away from sleep. He gets up and walks around the apartment, naked as a baby, looking at all the shit they've collected, the art, the tchochkes, the books. They pared down when they moved back to New York. They sold a lot of the art—all the expensive stuff they bought at auctions when the money was pouring like wine—a Picasso drawing, a large Paladino, a tiny Vuillard, a whole series of lithographs by Rufino Tamayo. They sold all that and kept their artist friends' paintings, most of them bought in the old days when they—and the artists—didn't have a pot to piss in.

Most of their books are gone, too. Who's got room for books in a New York apartment? You can have books or you can have a bed, take your pick. But they kept old scripts of plays they were in and he starts to go through them. Some go back to when they were in college, before they knew each other. Annie did *The Visit* when she was at Yale. The old Evergreen paperback script has her lines highlighted in yellow and her notes to herself in the margins. Diligent even then. He finds the script for the pilot of their TV show. Annie didn't want to do it; she thought TV was crap. But she came around eventually and they did the show and got rich and bought all those expensive paintings. And then the show ended and they got poor again and they sold the paintings. Who gives a shit, he says. Naked I came in and naked I go out. He gives his body a look and raises his eyebrows. He jiggles his package a little but there's no one home, so he decides to get dressed and take a walk. I'll walk until the sun comes up, he says, then I'll get a coffee.

It takes Annie nearly until dawn to get Olive to admit that her mother is not, in fact, her best friend. Once they clear that hurdle, the rest of the story tumbles out of her like a jackpot payoff in Reno.

"My dad died this year," says Olive, her tears now coming pretty much nonstop. "And . . . I don't know, it just threw me. I didn't even know he was sick. And then my singing . . . I couldn't sing anymore. I couldn't get breath."

"Were you close to him?"

"No. I mean, we were—but then he left us when I was fourteen and I wasn't allowed . . . to love him after that. My mother needed me to be for her."

Annie waits.

"I came home one day after my singing lesson. It was winter and dark out already. I walked into the living room and they were sitting there with all the lights off. My mom was on the edge of her chair with her head tilted a little to one side, like she was made of wax. My dad was leaning forward, his elbows on his knees, his face all wrinkled with worry. 'Your father's leaving us,' she said. 'For his secretary.'

"You know that mailbag that hangs on a hook at the railway station? It's just hanging there, blowing in the breeze? And then a train comes by and it's gone? Just like that."

Annie nods.

"He had courted me against my mom. My dad and I were in cahoots. We made fun of her behind her back—about how pretentious and arty she was and how she misused big words. And when he confided in me like that, I felt . . . so special, you know? My mother knew it, too. Oh my God, she was so furious. And the angrier she got, the more she drove him away.

"He hugged me the night he left. It was so . . . fierce; it pulled all the wind out of me. I could feel how much he loved me."

"You couldn't go with him?"

"She would have died. I know she would have. He knew it, too. He left me there for her. That night she was lying on the kitchen floor, shrieking and moaning; I didn't think it was ever going to stop."

"So you took care of her."

"Yeah, she said I was her rock. Still am."

"Do you love your father or do you hate him?"

Olive shuts her eyes tightly, but the tears find their way out.

"I don't know. He's dead now."

"It's no fun to be a rock, Olive. Rocks don't shine."

Olive just looks at her.

"How dare you shine? Does that about sum up your life, Olive?"

CHAPTER FOUR

WHEN CANDY COMES IN EARLY THE NEXT MORNING and sees Olive in deep discussion with her mother, she knows exactly who she is. She doesn't know her name or where she came from or how she got here, but she knows that this is the new girl, the new pretty girl. There's been a string of these girls going all the way back to her babysitters when she was a kid. She grew up and grew older but the babysitters always stayed around the same age until eventually they were younger than she was. They weren't all babysitters, of course. They were au pairs, secretaries, personal assistants, exercise coaches, and meditation teachers. Then, after Candy went off to college, they were cranio-sacral masseuses, past-life regression therapists, and tantric *dakinis*, but they were always around thirty-five and they were always great-looking.

They were there because Herbie and Annie liked having them around. Another woman in the house, one that wasn't her daughter or her mother, always worked out well for Annie. Another woman backed her up, saw her side of things, and she gave Annie additional ballast in the never-ending battle with the testosterone person. And Annie was secure enough to have another woman around—not only in her career and her position in the world, but secure in Herbie. She knew that although he'd flirt like crazy, sniffing up all those extra feminine pheromones that were flying around the house, his eye would always stay on the main chance. It was fun for her having Herbie jazzed like that, his balls clanging as he stalked around the house. So these girls were there for the juice really, extra household juice.

Candy went through every stage with them—jealousy, of course, sibling rivalry, rage—until she finally realized that they weren't her competition. She was, and is, the daughter. The girls weren't applying for that job. And she knew if she made a big issue and went to war with them, she would just get pushed further outside Herbie and Annie's magic circle. So she accommodated. She didn't like all of them—especially the New Age types who spouted inane jargon all the time—but some of them ended up being friends.

"Hi Mom," says Candy as she walks in on them. "I brought quiche." She holds her hand out to Olive. "I'm Candy. I'm the daughter."

"Oh, wow." Olive jumps up and shakes her hand. "I'm just . . . keeping your mom company. I'm Olive."

"Where did you come from, Olive? No wait, let me guess; you're an anesthesiologist; no, you're an alternative oncologist who has a new . . . no, you're too pretty. You . . . uh . . . you met Herbie somewhere and he wanted you to meet his wife. How am I doing?"

"I tend bar a few blocks from here. I met your father a couple of nights ago."

"Oh my God. That is too perfect. I'm speechless. That is just . . . too perfect."

"I'll go," says Olive quietly.

"No, don't mind me. It's just that I've . . . no, stay and have some quiche."

"Olive's a singer," says Annie, watching the scene.

Ah, thinks Candy, another artiste. "Oh yeah?" she says, plumping herself down on the bed. "What kind of singer?"

Showered, shaved, and caffeinated to the gills, Herbie shows up at the hospital around nine with the laptop Annie told him to bring. She wants to catch up on her correspondence, take care of business. When he walks into the room, there's Candy, Olive, and Annie sprawled on the bed picnicking on a bacon and tomato quiche that Candy bought at a fancy food store on Madison Avenue. All three girls look up at him like they know the face but can't quite place it. Candy holds out the box with the uneaten crusts of the quiche they've been devouring.

"Perfect timing, Pops. We were just talking about fathers."

Herbie turns back toward the door. "I have to get a haircut."

"No, stay. Olive needs an agent. I called Maurice and he's going to call Eliot James at William Morris as soon as they open. What time do agents get to work? Noon?"

Herbie finds himself, once again, behind the curve of the conversation. His mind is moving more along the lines of how does Annie feel; is she in any pain this morning; does she have any new thoughts about crossing into the great unknown—things like that.

"William *Morris*?"

"Maurice is very tight with Eliot James, who runs the place, doesn't he?"

"I thought you and Maurice were breaking up."

Candy gives him a look that says he understands nothing about life in sophisticated circles. "I imagine that's what's going to happen, yes. But we still live in the same house, you know. We're adults and we're very fond of each other. That didn't change. And I'm sure he'd love to show Olive how powerful he is, given half a chance."

"William Morris?" Herbie asks Annie, who, he must admit, looks perkier this morning.

"I don't think she should go with them. She'd get lost there—no matter how powerful Eliot James is. I think we should call Jeffrey."

Jeffrey Marshall has been Annie and Herbie's agent since they were just starting out in the early seventies. He championed them—each of them individually—when no one else would give them the time of day. It was never easy handling a married couple; most agents won't do it. Because if one of them is hot and the other not—a situation that repeated itself a hundred times over the years—you find yourself in the middle of a marital feud every time you call. But Jeffrey was always brilliantly diplomatic, reminding them that they weren't in competition, that they each had their unique gifts and that their careers would progress in different ways. Annie, he said, would hit first—she was dazzlingly beautiful and exuded that unbeatable combination of innocence and wantonness that would catch the eye of every director in town. Herbie, he said, would take more time. He was an Everyman, a clown, and his career wouldn't really take off until he was in his forties, at the earliest. He needed a little age, a little gravity, Jeffrey said, before the world would give him his due. In all this, he proved to be startlingly accurate.

In those days, most of the gay agents played it straight—suit and tie, the firm handshake, all sibilance banished from their speech. Jeffrey played the role perfectly. He was a handsome, elegant man-about-town, always with a beautiful woman on his arm at openings and parties. As charming as he was socially, he earned a reputation as shrewd negotiator with a killer instinct for getting clients the best deal. Over the years, as the world—

well, certainly the New York theater world—became more open about things, Jeffrey's true, extravagantly gay personality was able to emerge. Annie encouraged him from early on, supporting him to come out, to be himself, as she did with all her friends. Being who you really are is one of Annie's great themes. And Jeffrey treasured her for that. Now he's a foxy old queen who knows where all the bodies are buried from one end of the Broadway world to the other. He's also in complete denial about Annie's condition. Last week he called and said that he had something for her—a nice guest shot in a TV show—as soon as she's feeling better.

"Jeffrey specializes in old, washed-up people," says Herbie. "He wouldn't know what to do with Olive."

"That is so not true. He has a lot of young actors."

"You do realize that I didn't bring this up," says Olive. "Your daughter is a very powerful person."

Candy reaches over and squeezes Olive's hand. Annie, who's in the middle, touches both of them. They've bonded already, he thinks. They couldn't have been together—the three of them—for more than an hour because there's no way in hell that Candy got all the way uptown, shopped for a quiche and got over here before eight in the morning—so they've known each other an hour, tops. And they're friends forever. He hasn't made a new friend in forty years, he's thinking—not a real bosom-buddy kind of friend. Not the kind of friend he would recommend to his agent, for example. Maybe Maurice would qualify except that they move in such different worlds, on such different bank accounts; they end up dodging each other more than anything else. And when they do get together there's a discomfort, like they're both aware they're trying to make something happen that's not really there. The only friend he has—real, no-bullshit, everything-hanging-out friend—is Annie.

"What about your band?" he asks Olive. "Doesn't your band have an agent?"

"She doesn't have a band, Daddy. She just told you that to make fun of you. She does musicals and stuff. She's a singer-actress."

"She's done a lot," adds Annie. "Summer stock mostly, but also a show at Papermill Playhouse and . . . where else?"

"Goodspeed," says Olive.

"Goodspeed does great stuff."

Herbie nods and says that he'll call Jeffrey. There's another agent in the office—he can't remember her name—who knows all about what's happening with shows that use young people, which is about ninety-nine percent of what's being produced these days. Olive gives him her number and then puts her coat on.

"I'm out of here; this is family time."

"You haven't slept at all, have you?" asks Annie.

Olive shakes her head and smiles.

"Thanks for staying the night with Mom," says Candy. "That was great."

Olive, emotion surging up in her face, jabs her finger into her chest as if to say that she got more out of it than Annie. That she was the lucky one. She hugs Candy and they hold each other for a while. Then she sits on the edge of Annie's bed and takes her hand.

"I'll come back, if that's okay."

Annie opens her arms and they have a gentle hug. Then Olive crosses to Herbie and offers her hand, which he takes.

"Thanks, Mr. Aaron," she says. Herbie nods to her, feeling like the old dried-up piece of shit that he is. Mr. Aaron, my ass.

"She's special, Herbie," says Annie after Olive goes. "Jeffrey will be able to find work for her, you'll see. She has a truly wonderful voice, and she's drop-dead beautiful. She'll work."

Herbie nods. "There goes another good bartender." He plugs in the computer, which picks up the hospital's Wi-Fi signal, and he's in business. Word has gotten out about Annie's condition and the emails have been pouring in—not just friends and relatives, but cancer groups, hospitals, doctors, women all over the world who have had breast cancer and found hope in Annie's story. After her first bout in the eighties, she went public when nobody was going public; she stood up and spoke out and helped bring breast cancer out of the closet. Then twenty-three years later it snuck in the back door and sucker-punched her when no one was looking.

"Read me from the emails, honey," she says in a tired voice. Funny, he thinks, all the sparkle went out of her when Olive left.

"A lot of these don't need an answer—like the hospitals and the cancer organizations—they're all praying for you, thanking you for what you've done, shit like that."

"That's not shit, honey."

"No, I didn't mean shit; I meant stuff—you know—very nice stuff, but . . . you want me to read them all?"

"Forward them to me, Daddy, and I'll print them out. Then Mom can look at them when she likes."

"Read me the other ones—from our friends."

And Herbie starts to read. There are lots of friends—actors mostly, spouses of actors. Thirty-five years makes for a lot of cast parties. The funny people write funny messages despite the gravity of the moment; funny is the only way they've ever been comfortable expressing the truth—and their jokes, their sly, ironic allusions hit the mark. Candy, Herbie and Annie laugh and cry, hugs all around. Not a dry seat in the house, thinks Herbie. The sincere people's messages are breathtakingly sincere. With their hearts opened as wide as they can bear, they tell Annie how much they adore her and how much they're feeling.

Herbie is sinking like a rock. Each letter—each word—is like a claw in his chest, pulling him down. But he reads well, with emotion and clarity, like the good actor he is.

Annie, on the other hand, is having a ball, eating it up with a spoon. She's Tom Sawyer at the funeral. That she's the reason all these brilliant people dug deeply into themselves and came up with pearls is heaven to her. Once again, she's a Muse. Annie was always as much a Muse as anything else. Yes, great actress, mother, lover, wife, activist, feminist, yogist, meditatist, Pilatist—yes, great at all those things. But Muse is what she was born to do. Just hang out with her, you start looking at yourself again; you change something, you start something, you write a book, you lose twenty pounds. She doesn't even have to say anything—although she usually does.

"Now here's a strange one," says Herbie. "I wasn't even going to read it, but what the hell. From Bob, of course."

"Uncle Bob?" asks Candy. Herbie nods.

"Oh, let's hear from Uncle Bob," says Annie and she snuggles down in the bed like a twelve-year-old.

Bob Frankel goes back to their earliest days in New York. Annie did a play with him—Off-Off Broadway in a basement on East Fifth Street and Bob was brilliant in the play. He's a nervous actor; he's always worrying over every moment, but there's a terrifying honesty in all his work. He exposes himself in odd, funny ways and the audience can't take their eyes off him. In the play with Annie, he stole the reviews and brought so much attention to the play it almost moved uptown. Herbie and Annie used to drink with him after the show—although Bob, a rabid health nut, didn't really drink that much. Then Herbie got to know him better from the voice-over circuit, which was how they all supported themselves in those days. In between auditions or bookings, they would have lunch at one of those carts on Sixth Avenue—falafel or Thai food—and they'd philosophize. Bob always had an odd, often paranoid take on things and Herbie loved to provoke him and send him off on a rant. They'd argue merrily on the sidewalk for hours.

Bob was also blatantly in love with Annie. Head over heels. And he wanted to get to know Herbie so that he could find the secret—how could this guy get that girl? So Bob stuck around. They tried to fix him up once or twice, but he was—and is—too prickly for a relationship, and too needy at the same time—a great combination for seduction. They tried to add him to dinner parties but he was inevitably embarrassing, taking impossible, voluble positions on every issue, driving other guests into rages. But he never gave up courting Annie and Herbie—again it was that parental thing. He'd call the next day and sheepishly hint around about whether he had been obnoxious the night before and Annie would talk him down and then build him up again. While this gentle therapy was going on, Herbie would be pacing in the background, screaming, "Why does he have to behave like a fucking asshole all the time?" They put a lot of time and energy into Bob and ended up essentially adopting him. Yes, he's an asshole, but he's our asshole—like a puppy that never gets it right, that gets so excited when you come home it pees all over your shoe—eventually you learn to love him—kind of. Bob has been that kind of friend for more than thirty years.

"It's very short," says Herbie reading from the computer.

"Hi Darling, I just want you to know that you don't have to worry about me. I'm okay. I'm handling this. Love, Bob."

Candy falls back onto the bed like she's been struck by lightning. "Oh thank God! I have been up nights, pacing the floor. What if Bob Frankel can't handle this? Jesus, fucking Christ!"

"Everything happens to Bob," adds Herbie, laughing.

"No, it's great," says Annie, who would laugh if she had the energy. "Bob is Bob and I wouldn't want him any other way."

"Here's from Jim," says Herbie, looking at the next email.

"Oh," says Annie. "A poem?"

Jim is a poet. If you don't have a friend who is a poet, you might start looking around, because it's quite something to have.

"Yeah. It's called 'Five Charms In Praise of Bewilderment':

1

    After you leave for three days
I sit right down and start to write
    About the finer elements of silence
Lying through my teeth

2

    I have the vice

Of courting poems
    Pathetic, I know.
I also like to watch Oprah
    If no one is around to notice.
That's right,
    I court poems, I watch Oprah,
I even let out wordless sighs late at night,
    And call them
My spring fields ploughed, my ready earth.

3

    Sitting quietly at dusk, I'll admit

My life goes like this:
    Dark branches
Scratching the still darker window.

4

"How are you?"

I ask a woman at work.
    "I have no idea,"
she replies,
        sounding pleased with herself
at the heartfeltness
        of her bewilderment.

5

    We don't know,
can't possibly know,
        never have known,
never will know.
        We just don't know.

Three days later Annie dies. It's shortly after midnight and Herbie is beside her on the bed. She's in and out of consciousness and then suddenly Herbie gets a feeling in his spine like a buzzer went off. He puts his face next to hers and waits for breath and there is none. She's still warm like Annie. She smells the same, but there's no breath. He calls the nurse, who quickly affirms that Annie has passed. Herbie nods. The nurse waits for a moment, not knowing what he wants her to do.

"She's still here," he tells her. "Can you feel her?"

The nurse says that she'll give him some space and leaves the room. Herbie takes Annie's hand in his and holds it.

"You're here," he says. "You're still here."

She doesn't deny it.

Over the years, they didn't cling to each other; they were often separate. At parties, she'd go this way, he'd go that; but he always knew she was there. That's what this feels like. She's there.

He sits with her for a long time. At first he's just content. He's sitting with her; he's fine. Then he smiles. He can't stop smiling. He fills up with happiness that's unlike any happiness he's ever felt. It's more. It's euphoria. He feels like he's touching the edge of eternity. He feels like he understands all the mysteries. She's still here. This ecstatic state goes on . . . he knows not how long. It could be days. And then—suddenly, as if a switch went off—she's not there. He has no sense of her next to him. He looks around. He can't draw a breath. The silence bounces off the hard hospital surfaces. He touches Annie's face and recoils. It's not her. She's gone. He has to leave. He can't move.

"Your daughter's here, Mr. Aaron." It's the nurse, speaking softly, with a thick Queens accent like the Dingbat on *All in the Family*. Herbie turns to the door and there's Olive, coming to visit Annie after her shift at the bar.

"She's gone," he tells her. Olive freezes, knowing everything. She starts toward Herbie, stops and then runs down the hall.

"And now *she's* gone," he says, unable not to sound like Groucho.

All those years together he must have said a million times—honey, we should go. They're off to a show, the house lights are already dimming, they're thirty-eight blocks north of the theater and they haven't left the apartment yet. She's in her underwear and three or four possible outfits are lying on the bed. Honey, we really should go. She smiles at him and continues to put her look together, unhurried. She had her pace. They never missed a curtain. He looks at the empty shell of her body on the bed. He puts on his coat and goes.

CHAPTER FIVE

⌣

TWO WEEKS LATER THERE'S A MEMORIAL SERVICE AT the Booth Theatre on Forty-fifth Street. The Booth is an old gem, sitting right on the corner of Schubert Alley. It's a nonmusical house—only about eight hundred seats—and it's considered one of the desired places to mount a straight play on Broadway. Annie did a comedy there back in the early days and she's always had a soft spot for it. Her memorial is on a Monday, Broadway's traditional dark day, and it's a standing-room-only affair with friends coming from as far as London and Hollywood. It draws the cream of the crop—actors, writers, directors, and producers, all turning out to pay tribute to one of their own. Typically these show-business memorials are uplifting, lots of laughs, and happy memories as the speakers celebrate the life of the person rather than mourn the death, but today's service is having a serious problem getting off the ground. Yes, there are funny stories about Annie's early days—an actress friend shows a clip of a toilet bowl cleaner commercial that Annie shot when she was in her twenties; an actor reads a bad review she received from the *Times*, indicating that we won't be hearing any more from this sorry young ingénue—written, of course, by a critic who's never been heard of since; another actor recalls a ribald story about Annie's penchant for seducing the cameraman on whatever film she was working on.

But the show's not working today because of the all-encompassing black hole that is Herbie. The general consensus among friends and family is that he has been sedated for the service. What they don't realize is that none of them have ever seen him so completely unmedicated. He's off everything, no booze, no pot, no coffee—and he looks like he's been mummified, like one of those little dry Egyptians with crackly skin.

Candy, who's sitting at his side, tries desperately to pump some air into him, reminding him that Annie would want him to laugh, would want him to breathe, for Christ's sake. He smiles wanly and shakes his head in agreement, but there's no energy behind it. He always said that the problem with having a love affair like they had was that one of them is going to die first and then the other one is fucked. And that's what he looks like right now to Candy—fucked—with no hope of getting un-fucked.

"Maurice wants to take you to lunch, Pops. Why don't you do that?"

"What, today?"

"Yeah, right after. He wants to talk to you."

"No, I . . . I don't want to have lunch with anybody. Tell Maurice I'll be all right, don't worry."

They're walking up the aisle after the service. Herbie's nodding to people, not really looking anybody in the eye. He leans over close to Candy so that no one can hear. "So you and Maurice are working it out, or what?"

"I don't know about working it out, but he's been a prince these last couple of weeks, since Mom died. He hasn't taken his eyes off me for a second."

Herbie nods. "I'm glad to hear that." Some people are still milling around. It's around noon and actors have no idea what to do at that hour. It's like a crowd of vampires trying to stay out of the sun.

Herbie sees Olive waiting at the top of the aisle and he thinks she looks like the only one with light on her in the whole room. She and Candy have a hug and they make a plan to talk on the phone. Herbie watches them, thinking how did they get so close in so little time? Then Candy kisses him and says she's going to find Maurice and that he's going to take Herbie to lunch. He shakes his head in protest but she's gone. He sees Jeffrey, his agent, hanging back against the wall. Jeffrey's all in black—everything, shirt, tie, suit—all black—except for his face, which is gray. Jeffrey doesn't handle death well. Herbie waves him over.

"You look like a fucking mortician," Herbie says. Jeffrey grabs his hand and shakes it manfully. His breathing is shallow and sputtery, like an asthmatic having an attack.

"I'm not good at this, Herbie." He takes a few gulps of air like he's trying not to drown. "I'm not good at this. She was an extraordinary woman, and . . ." He gulps again.

"Jeffrey, Jesus Christ, don't do this. I don't need to hear this crap right now." Herbie takes Olive by the elbow and presents her. "This is the girl I called you about."

"Olive," says Jeffrey, as if he known her for years. "We've met, we've talked and she's already signed with the office. Hello Olive."

She says a quick hello to her new agent and then kisses Herbie gently on the cheek. "I'll talk to you soon," she says and disappears into the crowd.

"How did you meet her already? I didn't even tell you her name yet."

"Annie called me. She said she didn't trust you to do it. She said you weren't in very good shape, which is . . . obvious. She called me the day before she . . ." he pauses and starts to do the breathing thing again.

"Died, Jeffrey, the day before she died. It's all right; you can say the word. Jesus Christ."

"She told me she met an extraordinary girl and that I should sign her. And then, as soon as I can, I should get her cast in a straight play—a classic, preferably, so she has good words to say. Out of town, no money, it doesn't matter. She has to act, she said—really act, not the musical-comedy thing. I called Williamstown. They owe me. We'll see."

"She's absolutely right, of course." Herbie shakes his head and almost smiles. "She's still running things. To Annie, it doesn't matter that she's dead, she's still making things happen."

Jeffrey puts his hand on the top of Herbie's head in a fatherly, almost rabbinical way—a gesture unlike anything he's ever done before or ever will again.

"Take a tip," he says and makes his way out the door to the street.

Herbie bundles up, pretending not to recognize all his old friends and pushes his way through the crowd and out the door. He hits the sidewalk at a good clip and heads toward Eighth Avenue. It's cold but livable. His plan is to go up Eighth and then into the park at Fifty-ninth Street. Maybe he can walk this off. He starts to cross in the middle of the block and a limo almost runs his toes over. He lifts his hands up to the driver in the "what the fuck are you doing" gesture, and the back door of the limo opens. It's Maurice.

"Get in."

"No, I don't want to talk to anybody, Maurice."

"Get in the fucking car." He says this like a man holding a .52 Magnum to your nose. Herbie gets in the car. Maurice is on the phone.

"Hey, Bixby. I'm coming in, but I want you to cancel the whole day. Something came up. No, everything." He listens.

"No Bixby, I want you to cancel the whole day, which is why I just said cancel the whole day." He listens some more. "No, he just thinks he's important. Wedge him in tomorrow." Mrs. Bixby has been Maurice's executive assistant for years and can apparently do anything.

They ride up Eighth Avenue in silence, both of them staring straight ahead, watching the driver negotiate the traffic.

"Just drop me off at the corner of Fifty-ninth Street," Herbie says to the driver. "I'm gonna walk in the park."

"Just let me do this, will you, Herbie?" Maurice seems agitated, which is unusual for him.

"Do what?"

"I don't know, do what. But you're going to stay with me today and we'll figure it out, all right?"

"Candy put you up to this." Maurice doesn't respond and Herbie slouches down in the seat and steams like an eight-year-old.

Maurice Leventhal has been the smartest person in the room for as long as he can remember. He has a gift for scoping the system—whatever system it may be—and then, with ease, manipulating it to his benefit. School was a breeze—he never got less than an A and never studied more than a half hour per semester. Same with the SATs—he figured out what they were looking for and banged out perfect scores with no effort. That left him free in college to concentrate on girls and poker. Poker was an obsession. By the time he graduated law school he had stashed away enough tax-free money to bankroll his first business venture and he's been building on that ever since. He plays it all like poker—taking a long, objective look at his own position; then reading his opponent like the morning paper, cataloging all his weaknesses; then waiting patiently for the right moment to exploit the situation. He's never lost at poker and he's never lost in business.

With girls, however, it's been a different story. They just don't seem to follow the same pattern as normal people. And girls like him, which just makes it all the harder. He tries to play women like he plays poker, but it never comes out right—he wins every hand, he rakes in every pot and still finishes up the night a loser. He's baffled by women and he can't get enough of them, so he's pretty much been led around by his dick most of his adult life. By the time he met Candy, he'd been divorced twice and pretty much without hope of ever getting it right.

The limo drops them at Maurice's building on Madison and they take the elevator in silence up to a very high floor. Maurice ushers Herbie past the receptionist and back to his private office. Mrs. Bixby is on guard at her desk outside.

"Hello, Mr. Aaron. I'm very sorry for your loss."

Herbie nods and follows Maurice into the office, which is the size of Penn Station. There's a desk with absolutely nothing on it sitting in front of a corner bank of windows that has the whole city in its view—over Central Park all the way north to the George Washington Bridge if you look to the right; over the Plaza all the way down to the Statue of Liberty if you look left.

"What? You couldn't get a view?"

"You want a drink?"

"No. What time is it?"

"What difference does it make?"

"No, I'm not drinking today."

"Oh, that's like a rule?"

"What time is it?"

"Almost noon."

"Jesus."

Maurice picks up the phone. "A big pitcher of Bloody Marys, spicy—horseradish—you know. A quart of Grey Goose on the side. Two glasses. Fruit?" He gestures to Herbie who shakes is head. "No, no fruit." He listens and sighs. "Wedge him in, Bixby, wedge him in." He turns to Herbie. "You play basketball?"

"Never was my game."

"I'm going to change. Just make yourself at home. I'll be right back."

Maurice crosses to a door that leads to an apartment—bedroom, full bathroom with a Jacuzzi, a kitchen that's never been used, a big formal dining room, and a closet with about a million dollars' worth of clothes. Herbie wanders around the office, checking out the art on the walls. Maurice has a very sharp eye for art. In what seems like seconds, Mrs. Bixby appears with a tray—the pitcher of Bloody Marys, the extra quart of vodka and some sandwiches and chips. She puts them down on the coffee table and looks around.

"Where's Mr. Leventhal? Did he jump?"

Herbie smiles. Mrs. Bixby's sense of humor appeals to him.

"Do you need any help, Mr. Aaron?" He shakes his head. "I could twist the cap off the bottle for you, if you like."

"No, that's okay." Herbie pours a drink from the pitcher and tastes it. Then he adds a healthy slug of the vodka and stirs it in.

"It's never strong enough, is it? No matter how strong I make it, you guys have to add a little bit more." She pats him on the arm and leaves. Herbie tastes again. He has to admit it's a great Bloody Mary—spicy with lots of salt, black pepper, and horseradish and a serious kick of alcohol. And, oh yeah, tomato juice. He finishes the glass and pours another, topping it up with a glug from the bottle. Then he makes an identical one for Maurice and takes it into the bedroom. Maurice is checking himself in the mirror. He's dressed for the gym—except for the four-thousand-dollar black cashmere V-neck sweater that covers his

T-shirt. Herbie gives him the drink and they toast. "Here's to cashmere," says Herbie.

"Here's to a good day," shoots back Maurice. "First of many."

"Why not," says Herbie and they drink to it.

"You really don't play basketball? At all?"

"Actually I used to have a great two-handed set shot. Probably if I warmed up a little I could get that working again. But I don't run around or any of that shit."

"That's all right. We can play Horse."

"Where are we gonna play Horse?

"New York Athletic Club. We'll drop by your apartment so you can change. You have sneakers?"

"Yes, Maurice, I have sneakers."

Maurice sips his drink and Herbie finishes his. Maurice takes his glass and goes back into the office and makes him another one.

"You trying to get me loaded?"

"Yes, I am."

"You gonna take advantage of me?"

"That's right, Herbie. Four men are on their way up here. They're going to rip your clothes off and hold you down. Then I'm going to do everything I've ever wanted to do to you."

Herbie almost smiles. "So, this is widowhood."

At Herbie's apartment, Maurice can feel the sadness seeping through the walls. The apartment is spotless. Herbie's been holed up here for the last two weeks with nothing to do but clean. He comes out of the bedroom dressed in tan pants, a purple golf shirt and his own, much less expensive version of the black cashmere sweater. He has his sneakers on.

"Here, take a hit." He holds out his hash pipe to Maurice and lights the lighter.

"What's this?" Maurice knows full well what it is.

"Take a hit, Maurice. It won't hurt you."

"No, I don't do that shit."

'You never have? In college?"

Maurice shakes his head.

"Here, I'll hold it for you."

"It's illegal."

"I won't turn you in."

First Herbie demonstrates, taking in a lungful and holding it. Then he refills the pipe and passes it over. "Just take in a little. Otherwise you'll cough it all out."

Maurice takes the lighter and holds it up to the pipe. He takes a little smoke and immediately coughs it out.

"That always happens. Try again."

"This is fun?"

"Try again. Take less."

Maurice manages to hold a little smoke in his lungs and finally blows it out. "I don't feel anything."

"Yeah, yeah."

"I've led an exemplary life; I've built a fine career that I'm proud of, and now it's all going to come crashing down because of some degenerate actor."

Herbie takes the pipe, taps out the ash into the garbage and puts it in his pocket. "Maybe I should bring an extra pair of underwear. I hate walking around in moist shorts," he says as they're putting their coats on.

Mrs. Bixby, one step ahead as always, has transferred the Bloody Mary mix to a big non-drip travel pitcher that sits on a little coffee table in the backseat of the limo. There are two man-sized glasses, a full ice chest and the requisite new, unopened quart of ice-cold Grey Goose. The driver waits until they've made their drinks and then slowly eases the car in the direction of downtown. After half of his drink disappears, Herbie sets down his glass, refills the pipe and offers it to Maurice.

"Are you crazy?" Maurice points to the driver.

"What's his name?"

"Robert."

Herbie leans forward and knocks on the glass, which opens part way. "Robert, I'm gonna smoke a little medical marijuana back here. Perfectly legal. You got any problem with that?"

Robert smiles. "What's happens in the limo stays in the limo." And the glass slides closed.

By the time they get onto the basketball court, they're feeling pretty loose. They each pick up a ball and start to warm up on their own. There are a couple other pickup games on the floor but they have a half court to themselves. Maurice moves around pretty well, shooting one-handers and following with a layup. Herbie stands on the foul line and shoots two-hand set shots, one after the other. A two-hand set shot has not been seen on any respectable basketball court since the days when they played the game with an inflated pig bladder, but it's all Herbie's got. Maurice takes off his sweater and throws it on the floor against the wall.

"You want to go first?"

"No, you start." Maurice dribbles to his right, pulls up and fires a fifteen-foot jump shot. It hits the rim and bounces out. "All right, you have a free shot," he says.

"I know how to play the game." Herbie throws up his two-hander from the foul line and misses. "Gonna be a long day."

Maurice does the same thing as before, this time to the left, and hits it.

"Okay, you have to make that shot."

"I know how to play the fucking game, Maurice." He walks to the spot that Maurice let the ball go and throws up his two-hander, which goes in.

"That's not the shot," says Maurice.

"That's not where you made it from?"

"Yeah, but I made a completely different shot—dribble to the left, pull up and a one-handed jumper."

"You made the shot from here; I made the shot from here."

Maurice is laughing now. "You've got to be kidding."

"What, are you afraid, Maurice? That you're gonna lose?"

"Give me the fucking ball."

An hour later, they're in the car again, heading downtown to the Russian Baths. "I'm glad I brought another pair of underwear," says Herbie. "I hate walking around with wet shorts."

"Yes, you mentioned that."

"It's kind of a creed with me."

At the Russian Baths, they take a long steam and then go off to their respective massages. Herbie draws a 250-pound bald Albanian with hands the size of catcher's mitts. He gets pummeled for half an hour, then covered with kosher salt, which the guy rubs into every part of his body. The salt pulls out the toxins, the Albanian would say if he knew the language. By the time Herbie gets back to the steam room, he's almost sober.

"Now I know how a pastrami feels," he says when Maurice appears, also looking a bit wrung out.

"It's good for us. We'll live forever," says Maurice. They adjust their sheets around their private parts and get as comfortable as they can on the hot, hard tiles. They're the only ones in the steam.

"So," says Herbie after they sweat a little, "you're running around on my daughter?"

Maurice sighs a big one. "I thought you said you didn't want to talk about anything today."

"No, I said I didn't want to talk about me. You we can talk about."

Maurice stands up and starts to pace around the room. With the sheet he looks a little like Julius Caesar. "First of all, I'm not running around, as you well know. Candy's trying to push this girl at me, which is a fairly obvious way of telling me that she's done. That seems to be what's going on here."

"Would it make you feel better or worse to know that she's done this before?" Maurice stops pacing. "She's weaseled out of relationships before by lining the guy up with another woman. She gets unsure for some reason and then she tests the guy. So far, they all failed."

Maurice shakes his head sadly. "What we have is good. It's the best relationship I've ever had. We meet each other; we don't dish a lot of crap out onto each other. It's an honest, passionate relationship. What the fuck is she unsure about?"

"Candy's a little nuts is what. Maybe her parents fucked her up, who knows? But way down deep she can't believe the guy loves her. If you want to be with her, you have to ride that out."

"I just pretend this isn't happening?"

"No, don't pretend anything. Just accept it all. You have to take the whole package, Maurice. If you say, 'I really love this girl except for this one thing—if I could just change this one thing, then everything would be perfect,' then you've already lost her. Don't try to change anything. Accept the whole deal— her mood swings, her little neuroses, her fears—not only accept them—you have to love them, rejoice in them. You've got to say, 'there's my girl; there's my girl being herself.' Then you're a lover."

Herbie hasn't cried since Annie died, but he's crying now.

The sweat and the steam cover the tears, but Maurice knows he's not talking about Candy.

The two men continue their discussion on the nature of true love through a shared double porterhouse at Peter Luger, fueled by dry vodka martinis of an untold number. After that they go to a chic whiskey bar in Tribeca and drink grappa until the manager throws them out. When Maurice drops Herbie off, they hug in the street. He's going to make it, Maurice thinks, as the limo drives away.

CHAPTER SIX

"GOLF?" CANDY MAKES THE WORD SOUND LIKE SHE'S trying to bring up sputum from her lungs. She and Herbie are having breakfast at Barney Greengrass on Amsterdam Avenue. This has become a daily ritual—daughter checking up on father and vice versa.

"Yeah," he says, "I thought I would go work on my game."

"Are you serious? Golf?" If anything, she's even more incredulous when she says it the second time. Herbie just sits there, refusing the bait.

"You haven't played golf since you lived in Los Angeles, have you?"

"Once or twice."

"In fifteen years."

He nods. "But I've been watching them on TV, you know? And I think I've got it down now." Candy smiles and trowels some cream cheese onto her toasted bagel.

"Look," says Herbie, "I don't have a rational explanation— the other day I said to myself—the apartment, by the way, is becoming unlivable for me—it's . . . creepy in there—and I said to myself, what do you want to do? So that you don't go totally out of your fucking mind. And the answer was I want to play golf. I don't know why; I don't know where; I don't know who, but that's what I want to do. I'll take some lessons, I'll work on my swing, I'll play thirty-six holes a day, I'll get drunk and fall into bed. That's what I want to do. That's what I'm doing. Your mother hated golf. She said it took all day. Now I've got all day."

"Wow," says Candy, shaking her head in wonder. This is the most Herbie has said in one breath since Annie died.

"So I'm also thinking, what about you," he continues. "Are you moving out of Maurice's? Because if so, you can live in the apartment while I'm gone."

"You just said it was creepy."

"No, for me it's creepy. For you, it's . . . your parents' place."

"Way creepy. And I'm not moving out anyway."

"Oh?"

"No. We're . . . taking another look at everything."

"Ah."

The waiter comes and fills up their coffee cups. Herbie tucks into his lox-and-onion omelet and Candy watches him for a moment.

"So what did you guys talk about that day?"

Herbie shakes his head. "What happens in the limo stays in the limo."

The golf thing calls to Herbie from a long way back, from when he was eleven years old and his family moved a half block away from a public golf course. It wasn't much as courses go: it had bald spots all over the fairways that became mud holes when it rained and the clubhouse was just two unheated shacks joined together—one side was a locker room, but with some tables and chairs, a bar, and the starter's desk, and the other side was the pro shop. Even for a public course it was pretty shabby, but to Herbie it was like a get-out-of-jail-free card.

A schoolmate of his who lived up the street was a guy named Butch, who was a year older and well entrenched in the golf-course scene. Butch spent his summers being the cart-boy, a position of immense responsibility for a mere kid. He had to rent out the little red pull-carts for thirty-five cents a round and then wrangle them when they got returned and put them in to neat lines around the side of the pro shop. For this he made good money. Butch brought Herbie over and introduced him to the pro, who was a jolly Irish fellow with a red face.

"Well," said the golf pro, "we need a boy to shag balls. Are you interested?"

Herbie nodded although he had no idea what the man was talking about. Shagging balls, although it may sound like a medical condition for men over fifty, is a job on a golf course. It is the lowest job you can get. When the pro gives a lesson, he has a large canvas bag filled with old golf balls; he dumps them out at the spot where he's giving the lesson, hands the bag to a young boy—the ball shagger—who goes out into the field and waits for them to hit the balls directly at him. Then, if he's still alive, he picks up all the balls and brings them back. Herbie earned fifty cents an hour doing this and it was the first money he ever earned.

Then he got into caddying, which made him a little more money and also gave him a chance to get out on the course and learn the noble game of golf. He caddied for one guy, Stan, who taught him a lot of the basics. Stan always used a Spalding Dot golf ball and he would tee it up just so—with the word "Dot" right where the club was going to connect with it. Stan's wife's name was Dorothy.

"All right baby, here it comes," he would say and then he'd smack the living shit out of the ball. Herbie took careful note of the satisfaction on Stan's face after every drive. This was his first golf lesson.

Then he met Mr. Cole, who was a fixture around the clubhouse and as far as Herbie could tell, played golf every day of his life. He was an older gentleman with a pronounced limp and a flavorful Kentucky drawl. When Mr. Cole spoke, everyone and his brother stopped what they were doing and listened to him. It was rumored that Mr. Cole was a very wealthy man and that he slipped his caddy a brand-new five-dollar bill at the end of each round. Five dollars.

"Hubby, you big enough to carry mah bag? It's that big red one over theyah. Ah think it's bigguh than you are. Heh, heh, heh." All the men turned and looked at him and laughed, but Herbie knew an opportunity when he saw it.

"I sure can, Mr. Cole," he said, nervously eying the enormous golf bag.

"All right, Hubby, Ah tell yah what we're gonna do. See if you can hoist that suckuh onto one of them pull carts. Ah don't wanna kill ya the fust time out."

"No, I can carry it, Mr. Cole."

"You listen to me boy. You do as I say. Y'understand?"

"Sure Mr. Cole." And to the raucous laughter of the men in the clubhouse he lifted the big bag onto his shoulder and took it out to where Butch was tending the carts.

"That's Mr. Cole's bag," said Butch. Herbie nodded, staggering under the weight of it.

"He's gonna let you put it on a *cart*?" Herbie set the bag down on the cart and strapped it in securely. "Man, are you lucky."

Lucky, indeed. Herbie became Mr. Cole's steady boy. Not only did he earn five dollars every day that summer, not only was he able use the pull cart every day, but Mr. Cole also let him play a few holes once they got out of sight of the authorities at the clubhouse. Once Mr. Cole and his three cronies hit their drives, he would hand Herbie the driver and a brand-new golf ball and tell him to take a whack at it. Then he'd give him a tip about how to swing better and they'd all walk down the fairway together to their next shots. With the warmth of the sun on his head, the smell of the newly mown grass and the promise of a crisp new five-dollar bill at the end of the day, Herbie felt a stirring in his eleven-year-old chest unlike any feeling he had ever had.

That afternoon, he calls Jeffrey, who had left him a message. "Jesus, I got you on the first try," says Herbie. "Must be my lucky day."

"How are you?" There is still that funeral director tone in Jeffrey's voice.

"I'm fine, Jeffrey. The funeral's over, okay?"

"Okay."

"What did you call about? Not work, I hope, because I'm leaving town in a couple of days. I was going to call you. So all those wonderful jobs you were going to get me will have to stay on hold for a while."

"Where are you going?"

"Myrtle Beach, I think. In South Carolina. I'm gonna go play golf for a while."

"I've played there—when I was in college."

"You play golf?" There's as much disbelief in his voice as there had been in Candy's.

"Yes, I was actually captain of my college golf team in Wisconsin."

"How could I not have known that?"

"Are you seriously asking that? Maybe because you don't know anything about me. You never have."

Herbie thinks about that for a second and realizes it's quite true—except for the fact of Jeffrey's sexual preference, he really doesn't know a thing about his personal life. "Why is that do you suppose?"

"Hm. You're only interested in yourself, maybe?" He lets that sink in. "Annie knew everything."

"That you play golf?"

"That and everything else—that I have nieces and a nephew and what their names are; that I've taken flying lessons; that I only have one kidney; she knew everything."

"Jesus Christ."

"Annnnyway, that's not why I called," says Jeffrey, as anxious as Herbie to get out of this conversation. "I just want to report that our little condiment has an audition."

"Olive?

"Yes. A very nice one, if I may say so myself. *Uncle Vanya*, to play Yelena."

"Jesus. Where?"

"A regional theater—upstate. Tucked away where no one will see her."

"Good. That's good."

"But she wants to talk to you. I think she's a little terrified."

"When's the audition?"

"Friday."

"Sure, give her my number."

"Are you going to have your cell phone with you?"

"Yeah, yeah." Herbie is notorious for not ever carrying his cell phone.

"And you're going to turn it on? And recharge it every day?"

"Just tell her to call me, all right?"

Herbie goes to his optometrist and asks him to make a pair of glasses that doesn't have progressive lenses or bifocals—just his distance prescription. These will be his golf glasses. Then he goes to the pro shop at the Chelsea Piers driving range to see what the story is with all these new clubs that he's seen advertised on TV, hybrids. They're supposed to be for people like him, golfers who can't hit with the clubs they already own. He spends an hour test-driving the demo clubs, smacking balls into a big net that's been strung up in front of the Hudson River. Whenever he hits a good shot, he buys the club—conveniently forgetting that he's just hit ten bad shots with it a few minutes earlier. That's the secret to golf, he thinks, forgetting the bad shots. All I want to do, he says to himself, is swing away like I did when I was a kid. Just whack away at it without thinking about all that crap they tell you—one-piece takeaway, keep your head behind the ball, move your weight to your right heel, relax your hands, take a big shoulder-turn—Jesus Christ, it's a miracle you can stay on your feet after all that crap. I'm just gonna whack away at it like I did when I was a kid, swinging my arms in the sunshine. He leaves with four new hybrid clubs that he'll add to his old golf bag in the basement. He buys shoes, a glove, a couple dozen balls; he's outfitted.

Next he gets online and figures out where he's going to stay. He had been to Myrtle Beach once when he was in his twenties—with three other unemployed actors he played a weekly game with. That's what Myrtle Beach is all about—golf buddies who are looking for a cheap getaway where they can focus on the manly pursuits: golf, carbohydrates both solid and liquid, and a cheap, soft bed to crash in. Florida is for rich guys, whereas Myrtle Beach is for guys. He remembers a bar near the beach where a lot of golf bums hung out that had pretty good crab cakes. He rents a car for a month, books a room at a golf resort and makes an appointment for lessons with the pro. Then he calls his drug supplier and orders up a half ounce of weed. In fifteen minutes, the guy pulls up to the corner of West End

Avenue in a brand-new BMW and they consummate the deal. Now he's ready to go.

That night he's sitting at a bar on Amsterdam having the fried chicken special when his cell phone goes off. It's Olive.

"Hey," he says, "I heard you got an audition. Way to go."

"Yeah, I'm a little nervous."

"Hang on a second, I'm gonna go outside where I can hear." Herbie gestures to the bartender that he'll be back and puts his coat on and goes out onto the sidewalk. Amsterdam Avenue is nearly as noisy as the bar, so he huddles against the building.

"Why are you nervous? You've auditioned before."

"For musicals. This is completely different."

"Why?"

"There I just work on the music I'm going to sing. I know I can do the music. But with the acting, I don't know what they're looking for."

"Ah. That's just it—they don't know what they're looking for either. So your job is not to please them. Your job is to find yourself in her, in what's her name—Yelena."

"What do you mean?"

"What did you do before—when you had to read for a musical? After you did the singing?"

"I just said the lines so they made sense."

"That's it. That's all you have to do. And then don't forget you're her, not you. The sense that you make has got to be *her* sense. There's a place where that woman and the woman that's you come together. When you find that place, the lines will all make sense. You won't have to do a thing."

"But she never really says what she's thinking."

"Ah, so you're playing a woman."

"Very funny. But she's always tap-dancing, you know? So that people don't see the real her."

"Why?"

Olive doesn't speak for a moment.

"Okay," says Herbie pointedly. "Now you know what you have to work on. Call me as soon as you figure it out. I'm leaving town but you've got my cell phone.

"Where you going?"

"It's a long story. Go to work."

"No, where are you going?"

He sighs. He's tired of people being judgmental about his golf trip. "I'm going to play golf."

"I play golf!"

Herbie is speechless. She plays golf. Probably wearing those cute Bermuda shorts that tend to crawl up her butt a little bit and those socks that just cover her feet so that her ankles are bare. And a tight little golf shirt with the logo on her left breast, like the alligator is going to chew on her nipple. Oh my God. Women on the golf course have always generated a very powerful erotic charge for Herbie. A woman who would not be all that attractive under normal circumstances can take on pornstar status when she's swinging a seven-iron. It all started when he was shagging balls. There was an assistant pro named Rick, who was young and handsome and who hit the golf ball farther than anyone in the world. Rick gave all his lessons to women. They were lined up around the block. He actually did that thing where he put his arms around them from behind—to show them the rhythm of the golf swing. And from a hundred and fifty yards away, the young Herbie, carrying his canvas bag half full of golf balls, got a chubby watching them. It's been that way ever since—woman, golf course, chubby.

"Why don't you wait until after my audition and I'll play with you?" offers Olive, unaware of the erotic frenzy on the other end of the phone.

"No, this isn't a day trip. This is a falling-off-the-edge-of-the-world trip."

"Oh. Kind of a golf/suicide thing?"

He laughs.

"How's it been going?" she asks.

"Bad. It's going bad. I can't stay in my apartment anymore. Everything in there that used to make me happy now makes me sad. I think going away is the right thing."

"Where are you now?"

"At a bar, having a bite."

"Come over to my bar. I'll feed you."

"You're working?"

"Yeah, but it's slow. You'd almost be the only one here."

"What happens if you get the job? You'll have to quit the bar."

"It's my uncle's bar. He'll take me back. Come over; I want to see you."

Herbie pays up and grabs a cab to the East Side. Olive's bar has maybe a half dozen people talking and drinking and he heads up to his usual place—Siberia—where it's empty and dark. He watches her work for a while, notices her notice him, a little color coming into her face while she pours his vodka rocks.

"She's insecure is what it is," she says, putting down the drink. "She thinks people like her only because she's beautiful—not because of who she is. So she plays the role she thinks they expect her to play. She clowns and performs and . . . you know . . . tap-dances . . . to cover her insecurity, her fear—to cover that she doesn't know who she is either."

"Uh-huh."

And she's off again, back to the other end of the bar to get a beer for somebody. Then another couple comes in; they take their coats off, settle on the stools and order. It's a good ten minutes before she gets back to Siberia.

"And maybe that's the place where she and I come together, you know? I could definitely see myself that way sometimes."

"Uh-huh." He can see she's really into it now. "So what do you have to do for the audition? Read scenes?"

"Yeah, two scenes. I'm learning them so I won't have to look down at the script, you know? I'm just drilling them whenever I can."

"Maybe that's not a good idea."

She wrinkles up her forehead, a gesture that Herbie finds powerfully attractive.

"You can kill it that way. You're alone, looking in the mirror or walking around your bedroom, saying the lines over and over, repeating the same line readings and the whole thing turns into cement. You're frozen. By the time you walk in there, you won't be a human being at all."

"So I shouldn't learn the lines? I shouldn't work on it?"

"No, you work on it. But in a different way. Take her for a walk; take her shopping. See how she chooses a dress. Have her bartend for you tonight—see how she does it differently from you."

"I thought you said I should look for how we're the same."

"Yeah, that, too. Both."

"And I really shouldn't learn the lines?"

"You shouldn't decide how you're going to say them. That's the trap. If you're the person, then it doesn't matter how you say the lines. If you're her, however you say them is right. You could say a line six different ways on six different days and they'd all be the right way. Because you're her. I never learn the lines for an audition. Some people do. Some people do a whole, finished performance when they audition. I think that's jumping the gun. You're not ready to perform the role yet. You just started. It'll be weeks before it's time to make those kinds of choices. I think, anyway."

"So what do you do? When you audition?"

"I wing it. I go in with the script in my hand; I look at the guy or the girl I'm reading with—usually some assistant casting person—and I connect with him. Then I look down to see what I say next; I take my time; then I look up and try something— whatever pops to mind. But I'm really talking to that person in front of me—not to myself in my bedroom somewhere."

"So you just wing it."

"Yeah. Like I would do in rehearsal. Not jump to some performance before I know who I am and what I'm doing."

"Wow."

Herbie takes a long swallow of his vodka. "Of course, you should keep in mind that I never get work from auditions. I'm probably the worst auditioner in the history of the theater. If I got two jobs from auditions in the entire forty years I've been in the business, I'd be surprised. So, you know, take it with a grain of salt. A big grain."

CHAPTER SEVEN

THE NEXT DAY HE'S IN THE CAR, DRIVING SOUTH. ONCE he clears the Lincoln Tunnel and the oil refineries on the Jersey Turnpike, he opens the windows and the mid-March air hits his head like a leaf blower, blasting away all the dead and decayed shit he's been carrying around. Just moving, he thinks, is good. When he crosses the Delaware Memorial Bridge into Maryland, he can feel the tug of Baltimore, city of his birth, clotted with the memories of his dead parents, his troubled father, his troubling mother. He decides to take the beltway and skirt it.

His cell phone rings with that annoying jingle the phone company foisted on him. He's got to change that sometime, he thinks.

"Hello?" He says this in a whimper, as if to say please don't beat me. He hates the phone and all it brings.

"Where are you?" It's Jeffrey.

"I'm driving. This is dangerous. You know I can't do two things at the same time."

"Where?"

"What's the difference? I'm going seventy-five miles an hour; I can't talk on the phone right now."

"Did you tell Olive not to work on her audition?"

"What? No. Jesus Christ, I'm sure she didn't tell you that.

That is not what she said, believe me." He sighs. "You have misunderstood something that you have no right to get into anyway. This is about acting. You are about business. Stay on your side."

"I just got off the phone with her and she said you told her not to learn the lines."

"Stay out of it, Jeffrey. She'll be fine. You just find out when her appointment is, and where. That's your job. Jesus Christ."

"All right. Just drive carefully, will you? You're not going to try to get all the way there in one day, are you?"

"No, I'll stop in Virginia somewhere. When's the audition?"

"Tomorrow at five thirty."

"So she'll have to sit around and get tense all day?"

"Do you want me to find a place for you to stay in Virginia? I'll go online and call you back?

Herbie smiles. This is Jeffrey. The worrier. The fixer. "I'm okay, darling. Call me when she gets the part."

Every exit on the Baltimore Beltway is a memory—Falls Road, Stevenson Road, Reisterstown Road—and he's surprised that the memories are not all bad. When he gets to Liberty Road, he takes the exit and heads to his old neighborhood. What the hell, he thinks. Let's see if I can find the golf course. The car seems to know the way—a few one-way signs that weren't there before, but he finds his old house without a wrong turn.

It's a sad fucking house, he thinks, looking at it. A sterile brick box sitting on a tiny lot next to another brick box. Two bedrooms upstairs, sharing one little bathroom. The dining-room table downstairs, where once a month, after the dinner dishes were cleared away, his dad sat and paid the bills. He had it all laid out—his check ledger, his good pen, and a mountain of bills. From the living room Herbie watched his dad gnaw at his lower lip, his eyes cast down. And Herbie's mother baiting him, belittling him: "You couldn't have a shop of your own, could you? Because you're too afraid to try. My father had a shop—of his own. His own shop with his name on it. But you're too scared, little boy—little scared boy, shitting in his pants." His father never answered.

Herbie was her golden boy. He could make her laugh. He was her actor, even then. She enticed him with her attention just as she was humiliating his father. But that didn't mean she wouldn't turn on him, too—and when she turned she went low; she tried to cut his heart out. Herbie never knew which mother he was going to get. He knew she had a sickness. She couldn't help it. She died in a diaper, chanting nonsense syllables.

He sits in the car, looking at the house, and he fills his pipe and takes his patented one hit. Then he locks the car and walks down the street, past where Butch used to live, to the golf course, the playing fields of his youth.

The course is closed. There are no flags in the holes. There are some patches of snow here and there and the ground is still frozen. The old clubhouse shacks have long been torn down and replaced by a municipal-looking building, muddy yellow brick and dark green shutters. He stands on the first tee and thinks two hundred and thirteen yards, par three. Amazing that I can remember that, he thinks, given that I can barely remember how to tie my fucking shoes in the morning. He walks down the fairway to the green, thinking this was a hard shot for a kid—two hundred and thirteen yards is a long way for a kid to hit the ball. The second hole is across the street, so Herbie, nicely stoned at this point, takes his time and looks both ways before going over. Four hundred and ten yards, all uphill; par four. Another tough hole, he says out loud as he strides up the windy hill.

Annie was the only person he ever saw who could back his mother down. One time they were in Baltimore for a wedding and Herbie's mother was on her broomstick—she never handled parties well. They went to pick her up at her apartment and she wouldn't come down—something about how a friend of hers hadn't been invited to the wedding—some person they had never heard of—and she was in a fury. When Herbie finally got her in the car, she started ranting like a bag lady right in Candy's face. Candy was around seven or eight years old at the time and had never seen anything like it. Annie, her mother-lion instinct taking over, grabbed Herbie's mother by the shoulders and hauled off and belted her. Right across the chops. Herbie was shocked. But damned if his mother didn't calm down and start to behave herself. She always looked at Annie funny after that.

The second green is the highest point on the golf course. He stands there and surveys the whole course—except the part that goes into the woods on the tenth hole and comes out again at fifteen. Why, he thinks, would he keep this information in his head all these years? He has little enough storage as it is. Why does he still carry around a map of this place?

He walks back to his car, still stoned, and sits there staring at the house. He remembers how he used to hide in the coat closet downstairs—way in the back where no one could find him. He stood there perfectly still, taking in the smells of his father's topcoat and his mother's perfume. He waited there until he heard his mother calling for him. And he didn't move.

He starts the car and pulls out, makes a left at the golf course and heads toward Gwynn Oak Avenue. When it doesn't show up after a couple of blocks, he thinks maybe he passed it. It should have been here already, he thinks. I need to make a left and go down to Rogers Avenue—if I can find the fucking street that gets me there. He makes a left into a street that dead-ends a block later. He turns the car around and heads back but now he can't find the street he was on before. Just take a left, he thinks—any left will get you there. He's pissed at himself now and he pulls over. Take it easy, big boy, you'll find the street; you're fine. He sits there and waits for the panic to subside. By the time he gets back to the beltway the sun has set and everyone's headlights have come on. He gets onto 95 South, tucks in behind a station wagon going around fifty-five and takes it easy for a while. He never should have gone back, he thinks. He left when he was seventeen and that was the right move. His breath is coming normally now and he lets the miles drift by.

Herbie pulls off the highway south of Richmond and finds one of those cheap chain motels, beautifully situated across the parking lot from a bar with a piano player tonight. He checks in and showers. Then he calls Candy, who was worried about him driving. He tells her that he's off the road and safe and she thanks him. Then she tells him that she still can't figure out why he wants to play golf and he pretends to listen for a couple of minutes.

The bar is packed with Virginians, who seem to be relatively civilized people, and he finds a bar stool as far away from them as possible. He orders a sandwich and a double Maker's Mark over ice, being in the South and all. The whisky's good and he has some more. It reminds him how tired he is and exactly where he hurts. And it loosens up some memories.

He never worked in Virginia, but Annie did. She did a movie that kept her away for eleven weeks and the first three were in Virginia. He visited her on her day off and he knew the second he saw her that she was fucking around. She looked all lit up in that way that only good sex can make a girl look. They didn't talk about it then; he had his two-day visit with her and then he went back to New York for another eight weeks without her, knowing she was with another guy. Years later she told him about it. It was the camera operator. The guy had his eye glued to the camera lens and day in, day out he was gazing at her perfect face in close-up. Annie had the kind of beauty that deepened the more you studied it. He loved to look and she loved to be looked at—it didn't take long for it to go the next step. They did it in the camera truck during the lunch break. Herbie was never able to look at another camera truck without a huge sadness sucking him down—like a lead fucking weight hanging on his heart. "Fuck Virginia," he says as he polishes his drink, "and the horse it rode in on."

After three more whiskeys and the steak sandwich with fries, he makes his way across the parking lot and up to his room. When the phone rings two hours later, he could be on the moon for all he knows.

"Did I wake you?"

He fumbles for the light. "It's two thirty in the morning, for Christ's sake."

"I thought you wouldn't mind."

Herbie thinks about that and nods his head silently. He doesn't mind. "What's up?"

"Yelena tended bar for me tonight." Olive's voice is excited. "It was like you said—once I'm her I can do anything. I mean things were coming out of my mouth—I don't know where they came from. I don't talk like that."

"This is good."

"I got hit on like a hundred times. It was unbelievable. Girls, guys, the fry chef in the kitchen—Yelena's a trip."

"Doesn't Olive always get hit on?"

"Not really. Guys are usually pretty respectful."

"Because you're too pretty. It's intimidating."

"You're the only one I can think of, actually, who hit on me straight away." He can tell she's smiling.

"Really," he says, drily.

"Anyway, I more than doubled my tips tonight."

"You should split it with her."

"And it was Yelena who called and woke you up, not me. I never would have done that."

"Tell her she has to be careful with an old man. No sudden moves or surprises."

"Don't give me that old man crap."

"Who says? You or her?"

"Me."

He props his pillow up and leans against it, getting comfortable. "So, tomorrow at five thirty. What are you going to do all day?"

"I'll go shopping with Yelena, I think. Except that she'll be extravagant. She's a spender, definitely."

"You going to work on the scenes?"

"I'll go over them some. I'll be ready. I feel good about this."

Herbie smiles on the other end.

"What about you? Are you very lonely?"

Lonely? It's like he's falling, endlessly, in a place with no light and no air. He has no idea if he's falling up or down. It's just panic and hopelessness and dread.

"I just keep thinking she's in the other room, brushing her teeth or something. And I'll look up and there she'll be."

"Hang in there, coach," she says, softly.

CHAPTER EIGHT

HERBIE HITS MYRTLE BEACH AT THE APEX OF A TRIPARtite convergence—spring break, St. Patrick's Day, and the annual National Shag Dancing Competition, all happening together, all happening today.

"This is why you should check with a travel agent," he mutters as he inches his car through legions of half-naked, drunken college students with green plastic shamrocks on their heads. "There go the bars," he says out loud. "Fucking amateur hour."

He makes his way to his hotel, which is really more like a golf resort, with three separate courses—all named for celebrity golfers—a golf school, restaurants, and shops. It's called St. Andrews, which gives you an idea of how pretentious it is. He drives up to the ornate reception area—a third-rate version of a Vegas hotel—and there's a place to drop off his golf bag so they can take it down to the golf area and he won't have to put it in his room. They frown on golf clubs in the room. He pops his trunk and an eager young fellow takes the bag out of the trunk. He has a bit of a sneer on his face as he lifts Herbie's canvas golf bag with its motley set of clubs and sets it on a rack next to a dozen hefty leather bags with gleaming matched irons and fluffily head-covered woods.

"They're collectibles," he tells the kid. "Be careful, they're worth a fortune."

"Yes sir. Polish 'em up for you?"

"No, no. They look just the way they're supposed to look."

After he checks in, he follows another tanned young fellow through endless corridors to his Golf Package Suite. He tips him and as the kid lets himself out, the click of the closing door hits Herbie like a brick. How many fucking hotels, he thinks. On location in some half-assed city, shooting some dreary fucking film, away from Annie, away from my life. The only thing to do on location was to find someone to have sex with as soon as possible—some actress or, more probably, her stand-in. Someone who likes to drink, preferably. It's not adultery on location, as the old saying goes. Annie had her flings, too. Not as many—just three—that cameraman in Virginia and two actors. But when she had them, they were doozies, with feelings and emotions—unlike Herbie, who would have done it with a goldfish if that's who was around.

They told each other about all their affairs one afternoon in a course they were taking in Northern California—some New Age communication course—and they spilled everything, secrets they thought they would take to the grave. Annie only had her three, but Herbie's list went on and on—women they had both worked with, a friend of Annie's, some hookers in Vegas— his confession went on into the evening. In the end it was Herbie, of course, who was devastated. It took him months to get over it. But finally, they both realized they felt better being clean with each other, so they decided to keep it that way. After that, the only fucking around they did was together.

Herbie unpacks and puts on his golf clothes, which remarkably resemble the clothes he was driving in: tan pants, a white polo shirt, and a black cashmere sweater with the sleeves rolled up. He has his first lesson in half an hour. Good, he thinks. Take my mind off.

He meets the golf teacher outside the pro shop—tall, tanned, sun-bleached blond hair, a little older than the car valet and the bellboy, but not much. Herbie notes how they all have blond hairs on their tanned, ropey arms.

"Well," says the boy, looking at his clipboard, "how about we get right down to it, Mr. A-Ron? Ready to hit a few golf balls for me?"

"Actually Dan, I'd rather . . ."

"That's Don." He holds out his hand. "Don Merritt, Mr. A-Ron." He shakes Herbie's hand forcefully, as if to make him remember the name.

"Mister what?"

He checks his clipboard again. "You are Mr. Herbert A-Ron, are you not?"

"Aaron. Aaron. You never heard that name before?"

"I certainly have. It's in the bible. A-Ron was the brother of Moses."

"You a Mormon?"

"Uh, no I'm not."

"Aaron. It's pronounced Aaron."

"I'm sorry, Mr. . . . Erin? How 'bout if I call you Herbert? Or Herb?"

Herbie nods vaguely. He hates this kid. "Look, here's what I want to do: first I want to sit down with you at the bar and I'll explain exactly what I'm looking for here. Otherwise we're just gonna waste a lot of time, okay?"

"The *bar*?" Don's voice is up an octave now. "Ha, ha, no, I don't think we can do that, Mr. A-Ron. Oops, sorry." He laughs. "But that's just the way we *say* that name down here. I'll get it." He laughs again, manfully. "No, we can't, uh, we can't go to the *bar*. My boss would not look kindly on that. No he wouldn't."

"Here's the deal, Dan. I don't want your standard golf lesson. I've had many, many golf lessons and believe me, they're worthless. For me, I mean. For everybody else, I'm sure they're fine. So what I want to do is sit down with you—it can be at the bar or not at the bar—and tell you what I'm looking for here, okay?"

Don takes a moment surveying the driving range, like he's looking for spiritual help; then he looks at Herbie and purses his lips. "All right, tell me."

"I want you to help me work on my swing—*my* swing, not your swing—without all the mishigas."

"The what?"

Herbie sighs a big one. "Mishigas. It's a Yiddish word. It means, like, a lot of nonsense or the whole rigmarole, you know?"

"Sir." Don's all fluffed up now, like a gamecock. "The Nine Secrets to Power Golf is not *nonsense*." He declares this fervently. "It is not a rigmarole or a . . . mitchicass. It is science, sir. Pure, tested and proven science. And it has helped many, many golfers to a more successful and pleasurable golf game."

"Look . . ."

"The Nine Secrets to Power Golf was created by Mr. Mac McFeely, who is without a doubt the finest teacher for the higher-handicapped golfer—I think—in these United States."

"Look, Dan . . ."

"Don, goddammit!" He hangs his head like a puppy dog. Then he starts walking in a big circle, head still down, his ears all red. Herbie muses on how blond people's ears turn red when they get mad. "I'm sorry, sir," says Don finally. I'm getting a little sore here."

"Don, Don, my son. You have to understand something: I

can't remember nine secrets to anything. I can't remember two. I don't want secrets. I just want to hit the fucking ball."

The lesson proceeds downhill from there. Don, in an effort to change the air between them, suggests that he videotape Herbie as he hits the ball. This is not a good idea. Herbie launches into a diatribe about how he never watches himself on film—that it's the very death of his creative process; it makes him self-conscious and therefore unable to be his free and instinctual self. Don looks like he's in a nightmare, unable to understand a word of what he's hearing. Herbie could be speaking Farsi, for all he knows. The lesson ends in the pro shop with Herbie trying to get back the money he paid for the other eight Secrets to Power Golf that he's never going to learn. Finally he and the head pro negotiate a deal for half and neither of them feels very good about it.

Still steaming, he goes to his room, showers and puts on his drinking clothes, which are very similar to his golf clothes. Then he goes to the bar and finds his spot, separate of course from all human contact. The bar has one of those "nineteenth hole" motifs and he's in no mood for it. "A bar should look like a fucking bar," he says to the approaching bartender. After he downs his double mojito—for some reason, he's decided that's the appropriate drink—he surveys the room and sees, in a dark corner, Don, the golf teacher, pouring his heart out to a preppy-looking young woman. He gets another drink and carries it across the room.

"If we had started here, like I said," he says to the miserable young man, "none of this would have ever happened." The girl instinctually moves her chair back, preparing for a fast getaway. "This is a good life lesson for you: when a drunk suggests you go to the bar first, listen to him. He knows of what he speaks."

Don looks up at him warily.

"You got blindsided. You didn't do anything wrong; you just walked into the wrong guy at the wrong time. Here." Herbie puts a hundred dollar bill on the table. "Get drunk and forget about it. You're a good kid." Then he winks at the girl, who blushes, and goes back to his spot at the bar. He's got to revamp his plans, he thinks. First he's got to get out of this phony, tarted-up Holiday Inn and find a simple place with a good bed. Then he's got to find a real bar.

It takes him about an hour to locate his car in the vast parking lot. This is not helped by the fact that he can't remember what kind of car he's driving or what color it is. "You are one sad fuck," he says to himself when he finally gets into the car. He fills his little pipe, takes a toke and puts the car in gear as he lets out his breath. Let's cruise this town, he thinks.

Once he nears town, he can barely move because of the drunken children, would-be Irishmen and Shag dancers. But he's happy to go slow. He needs to calm down. Then his phone jingles.

"Where are you?" It's Olive.

"Driving around. It's spring break—you wouldn't believe this fucking place." He listens to Olive smile. "So, how'd it go?"

"Really good, I think. I got a callback." There's lots of excitement in her voice.

"Already?"

"Yeah. About an hour after I got home, Jeffrey called and said they loved me and they want to see me again tomorrow."

"Why?"

She can tell he's not happy. "Why do they want to see me again?"

"Yeah."

"Because they liked me, no?

"Then let them hire you. Callbacks suck. They're a brilliant way to lose a part that they already want you for. Just tell Jeffrey to tell them to make you an offer. See what they do."

"I don't think so, Herbie. I'm gonna to go back. I won't lose it."

"Do what you want."

There's a long silence while Olive listens to him drive through the crowded streets.

"Let's talk later. When you're not driving, okay?"

"Fine."

"Take it easy."

"Yeah, yeah."

He punches the disconnect button and feels himself filling up with anger again. He can't lose it today. He speed dials Jeffrey, who starts right in about the callback and how great it is. Herbie cuts him off.

"What did they say?"

"They want to see her again tomorrow."

"Yeah, I know that part, but what did they say? How did they say it?"

"I only spoke to the casting person and she said, where did this girl come from? Where have I been hiding her?"

"She said that?"

"Yeah."

"So they want her. It's over. They're pregnant. Have them make an offer."

"You've got to be kidding! No one's ever heard of her. They want to make sure. They might want to line her up with some of the other people—make sure they all look like they belong in the same play. You know what they do."

"Yeah, they jerk themselves off."

"If that's what they want to do, that's what they do. She's

going in at ten thirty. If they want her to jump through hoops, she'll jump. That's show business."

"Don't fucking tell me about show business. Your job is to represent her, not them. Do your fucking job."

Jeffrey hangs up on him. Herbie's too mad to drive, so he puts the car in the first lot he sees and walks toward the beach. It's chilly, maybe around fifty degrees, and he can't understand why everybody wants to have their shirts off. Fucking kids think they're going to live forever.

He passes a bar that he thinks he recognizes from back in the days when he thought he was going to live forever. They had good crab cakes, he remembers. He goes in and wrestles himself some space at the bar—forget about getting a stool—but he manages to get one elbow on the bar and that's enough to establish a beachhead. He can hold this spot all night if his legs hold out. He orders his double mojito and a crab cake sandwich and tries to negotiate a little more room by shoving his hip into the guy next to him.

"Easy fella. There's room for everybody," says the guy, whose belly is taking up at least three spaces.

"Yeah, sorry," says Herbie. "I'm getting a sandwich. So I need a little room."

"No problem. You in town for the golf?"

"No, I'm a shag dancer. I eat to keep my strength up."

The guy thinks this is hysterical. He grabs the guy next to him by the shoulder. "I ask this guy if he's here to play golf," he screams over the din, "and he tells me he's here for the shag dancing." They both think this is the funniest thing they ever heard and they both tell it to a third guy, who's one stool down. "He's got to keep his strength up!" A whole new round of laughter.

The three guys are down from Southern Ohio for a week away from the wives. Their faces are the color of dried blood from the sun and the drink.

"So, seriously," says the fat one, "you play golf?"

"Not for a long time, but I'm here to, you know, takes some lessons, screw around."

"Which one? Take some lessons or screw around?"

Herbie shrugs. This is more social contact than he's had in a while.

"Where you from?"

"New York."

"The city?"

"Yeah."

"My wife drags me there once a year—to see the shows—but I could never live there. Too crazy for me."

"It's a lot safer than walking around than this fucking place. You could get raped by a leprechaun."

This brings another round of laughter as the big guy repeats the joke to the other two. Herbie signals the bartender that he's buying drinks for everybody.

"You want to play tomorrow? We're going off Pine Tree Hill at nine forty—best public course in America."

"Sure. Sounds good."

"Thirty-five bucks you can play all day."

"I'll be there. You might have to be a little patient with me; I haven't played in years."

"Oh Christ," says the big guy, "you'll fit right in. I just had my hip replaced and they gave me one that doesn't know how to play golf for shit." Laughs all around. Then the guy in the middle says that he has that disease you see on TV where he has to pee every five minutes, so his game is not what it used to be because his concentration is off. And the third guy, who's quieter than the other two, says that he's really a tennis player and doesn't know much about golf at all.

"You're probably the best golfer in the bunch—don't worry," says the big guy. "What's your name?"

"Herbie."

The guy points to his chest first. "Bill, Alan, and Bud, whose real name is Charles." They all shake hands and the drinks come, along with Herbie's crab cake. He takes the top piece of bread off and cuts into the cake with a fork, where he finds little bits of red and green pepper mixed in. He calls the bartender back.

"Why do you have all this shit in here? A crab cake is crab—just crab. It's not a fucking salad."

The guys—his new buddies—find this hysterical. The bartender, who's about the same age as the kids out in the street, doesn't know what to do.

"Do you want something else, sir? A burger?"

"No. Just give me the check."

He pays up and tells the guys he'll see them in the morning. This has been altogether too much human contact for one day. When he gets back to the room, he turns the TV on; then he turns it off; he paces for a while, talking himself down. Then he dials Olive's number.

"Hey, Grumpy," she says.

"You at the bar?"

"No. I took the night off to work on my audition. Ten thirty tomorrow."

"Yeah, I know. Don't let them put you through any shit."

"I won't, but why would they?"

There's no response from Herbie.

"Why are you so weird about this? What is it about callbacks that makes you so pissed off?"

"Callbacks are a rigged deal. They're about *his* insecurity —the director's. He liked you but he doesn't trust himself—

probably because he knows he doesn't have any fucking talent—so he wants you to make him feel better."

"Okay, so I'll make him feel better."

"It's not okay. It's a false situation. He doesn't need to see anything new or different from you—he just needs somebody to pat him on the back and tell him he was right the first time. But that puts you in an odd position: do you repeat what you did the day before? That's no good because repeating is bad acting. Do you show him something new? That's dangerous because the only reason you're back is that he liked what you did the first time. So what do you do? I went up for a TV pilot once—years ago—and did a good audition—right off the top of my head, of course. And they asked me to fly out to L.A. to read for the network. So I rehearsed the scene hundreds of times, working it to death and I went in and stunk up the place. The director, the guy I read for originally, comes out afterward, hysterical. 'What happened?' he says. 'Where was the guy I saw last week?' I'm not good when I do that. Every time I tried to over think it, work it out in my mind—I fucked it up. Not just acting—with everything. After sixty years of this shit, I finally learned to trust it."

"Your instinct?"

"Yeah."

"So what's your instinct for me tomorrow?"

"Okay; first, you should go in and tell the director to grow the fuck up."

"Gee, that sounds like a great idea. Are you stoned?"

"Yeah."

"Hang on a second."

Herbie can hear her walk across the room and open a drawer. Then, after she fumbles around a bit, the sound of the cigarette lighter and a big inhale, a long pause, then the exhale.

"I only need one hit," she says with a scratchier voice.

"Me, too."

"Really?" There's a long pause as they think about this phenomenon.

"So, I get that the director is insecure, so he needs to make sure I'm good, but I don't understand why you get so angry about it."

He doesn't answer for a while. They listen to each other breathing.

"I'm angry because my life is over. I had a brilliant life and it's over. Every day it gets worse. I don't know . . . how to talk, how to relate to people. I don't know how to fucking breathe anymore. And I can't . . . right myself, you know? I'm like a little baby; I tipped over in my crib and can't set myself up again. I'm waving my arms and I'm screaming my head off, but there's nobody who can set me up straight again."

Olive is crying.

"What are *you* crying about?"

"I'm sorry."

"Oh Jesus. If you want to cry, then fucking cry."

Olive takes a moment to pull herself together.

"I think what you have to do is help me, Herbie. I think that's why I'm here."

He grunts.

"Annie made me promise to call you when I needed help. She said you're the best in the world. The best. So help me, Herbie. Tell me what to do."

He's silent.

"If you had a callback tomorrow, what would you do? I mean after you told them all to go fuck themselves? Then what would you do?"

That gets a smile. "Maybe I'd ask the guy to direct me—

have him tell what he thinks is going on under the scene, you know? Some subtext. And then I'd take the adjustment and go back on instinct. Then at least I could be a good actor."

"That's pretty brilliant."

"Yeah, because he'll feel like a good director when you make the adjustment he asks you for—so then he can relax and just cast the play and stop jerking himself off. That's all this is really about—making that poor shmuck feel better about himself."

"How do I get him to direct me?"

"Ask him."

"Just like that?"

"Yup."

"I'll try."

"Don't try. Do it."

"I will. Annie was right. You're the best."

There's a pause. "Sometimes it feels like she's still here."

"Is this one of those times?"

"Yeah."

"Maybe you could think of that as a good thing?"

He is silent.

"Good night, Grumpy."

"Good night, Dopey."

CHAPTER NINE

O LIVE GETS THE JOB, OF COURSE. AFTER SHE AND THE director work for the better part of an hour on a scene from the play, he crosses to her with his arms open wide and a warm smile on his face.

"Lovely. Welcome to the cast," he says with a very charming East End London accent. Then he takes her by the shoulders and places a chaste kiss on the top of her head. The producer and the casting people stand and give her a hand.

He's nothing like Herbie said, she thinks. He's not stupid or untalented or insecure. He's really great—generous and patient, completely open to new ideas, and not altogether bad-looking. Just stay calm. Just smile and thank them all and get out of the room without tripping. I got it, she thinks, her heart leaping out of her body. I got the part. I'm in the play.

As soon as she hits the street, she calls Jeffrey, who's ecstatic.

"This is a lot more important than you know, Olive. Because it's Chekhov and because Sam Harding is the new *enfant terrible* in London, some very good people are doing this. You'll be in excellent company, my dear."

She stops in the middle of the sidewalk on Forty-eighth Street and a sudden chill hits her spine. Now she actually has to go into rehearsal with all these pros—in three days—and act

Chekhov. What happens when they find out she doesn't know what she's doing?

"Hello? Darling, are you still there?" says Jeffrey on the other end. "Earth to Olive—come in please."

She tries to calm her breathing. "Yeah, I'm a little nervous all of a sudden."

"Of course you are. Who wouldn't be? But as soon as you start in, as soon as you get to the work, you won't have time to be afraid. Remember, they chose you because they thought you were the best."

"They chose me because Herbie told me what to do. He set me up so that I couldn't fail."

"Look, darling, Herbie's very smart and he's Svengali with pretty women, but he didn't go in there and get the part; you did."

"I have to call him."

"Good. Then call me back. We'll go through all the logistics—travel, accommodations, per diem, all that. You leave in three days. You'll be making scale—minimum salary—as will everyone else; alphabetical billing. Welcome to the world of serious theater, Olive."

She speed dials Herbie and gets his voice mail. Come on, Herbie, she thinks. I need you.

He, alas, couldn't be farther away if he were in Tasmania. He's on the seventh hole of the Pine Tree Hill golf course, flailing away with his drinking buddies from the night before. And as bad as his game is—he's rusty and stiff and in dire need of Advil—he's still the best of the bunch. Bill, Alan, and Bud are beer-drinking golfers. They've already worked most of the way through two six-packs and they're planning on restocking at the turn. They carry dozens of balls in the cart and whenever they hit a bad shot—which is always—their rule is to just drop another ball and try again. The question of putting, the most psychologically stressful part of golf—especially for men of a certain age whose testosterone no longer impels them to strike the ball without fear of failure—has been resolved by Bill, Alan, and Bud with another rule of their own devising: if your ball rests more than six feet from the hole, it's an automatic two-putt; within six feet, it's a gimme. Putting? No problem. Herbie is deeply impressed by how, with these tiny, subtle changes in the rules, his score is improving at an amazing rate. He makes a mental note to bring more golf balls tomorrow. With an endless stock of balls, he'll be breaking par in no time.

When Olive gets back to her apartment, she tries him again but has to leave another message. "Herbie, it's me. I got the part, but I'm getting worried. I really need to talk to you. Maybe you could even come back here before I have to go so you can work with me on it? Just call me, okay?"

She takes down a suitcase and starts to pack. It's cold up there. Rochester. Where the hell is Rochester, exactly? She stops packing and picks up the script for the play. She stares at the page for an hour, but nothing makes any sense. She goes back to packing when the phone rings.

"Herbie?"

"No darling. Jeffrey. I thought you were going to call me."

"Sorry. I'm waiting to hear from Herbie."

"We have a lot to talk about, but first I have a request for your phone number from your new director. May I give it to him? He wants to talk to you about the possibility of using another translation than the one you have."

"Another translation?"

"From the Russian. Apparently they have a new one, done by a Brit playwright named . . . wait a minute . . . oh dear. His name is Hassam Taamzi. Doesn't sound very British, does he? Anyway, Sam Harding thinks it's great and he wants to talk to you about it."

"Okay."

"I can give him your number?"

"Sure."

"Then tomorrow you'll drop by the office. I should have the contracts by then and I can give you all the logistics. Tomorrow, around eleven?"

"Okay. See you then."

"Why do you sound sad, darling?"

"I don't know. I want to talk to Herbie."

. . . Who has finished his round and is now holding forth in the clubhouse bar, working his way through a series of vodka and tonics and scarfing down a shrimp po'boy with fries. Herbie has the kind of metabolism that slows down after a big meal, so he tries never to eat until after his workday is finished. Which means when he's doing a play, he doesn't get to his first real meal of the day until around 11:15 at night. Now he's buying drinks for his merry golf pals and a few other duffers who have wandered over to their table. One of them had recognized Herbie from TV and came over to confirm. Herbie hates this particular aspect of his profession like a cat hates water.

"Are you that guy? You look like that guy."

Herbie nods, warily. "Yeah, I'm probably that guy."

"Bullshit." This is said with equal stress on both syllables.

Herbie smiles. "You're right, I just look like that guy."

"No, bullshit, you are that guy. Now that you talk I can hear it. What was the show?"

Herbie says the name of the show and the guy tells him he's right. Then he starts to call out to his pals at the other table and Herbie takes him by the arm.

"Do me a favor, pal. Can we keep this, like, just between us? Otherwise . . ." He makes a vague gesture in the air. The guy's eyes narrow and he puts his paw on Herbie's shoulder, draws him in and directs his beer-soaked breath straight up Herbie's nose.

"Don't say another word. I understand." And then he does that thing with the pretend zip locking his lips.

So now Bill, Alan, and Bud, plus the guy with the bad breath and his friends are all around the table watching Herbie eat. They're talking golf.

"You know, Herbie," says Alan, "you mind if I give you a little tip?"

"About my golf game?"

"No, about your sex life." Big laughs all around.

"You're going to give me a tip? With the way you swing a golf club?" Alan holds his hands out and shrugs. Why not?

"Sure" says Herbie. "I sit at the feet of the master. Tell me."

"All right, I will: your practice swing is completely different than your actual swing at the ball. Radically different. Are you aware of that?"

Herbie looks down. His chins are piled up on his neck and his lips are tight in the expression of "somebody better restrain me." He holds this pose for a long, dramatic beat.

"Alan, I am aware of that. I was once on a golf course—a long time ago—and some shmuck, who was over in the other fairway playing another hole entirely, drives his cart all the way across the fucking golf course just so that he can impart the same piece of wisdom that you just gave me. 'Do you know that your practice swing is completely different from your real swing. It's like Dr. Jekyll and Mr. Hyde,' this guy said."

"Well?"

"I killed him. Right there on the eleventh fairway. I took out my sand wedge and cut his fucking head off."

In the meantime, Olive gets the call from her director. Could we talk about this over dinner, he wants to know. I'd like to give you a copy of this new translation and show you why I like it so much—especially in terms of your character. They make a plan to meet at eight o'clock at Joe Allen, which is one of the stellar theater bars in the Broadway District. Olive is beaming again, all fear banished for the moment. She's been to Joe Allen before; she's watched famous Broadway actresses having late suppers with their agents or better yet huddling over a script with the director of their new play. Now she's the actress. She calls Jeffrey just because she has to tell someone.

"Is this kosher? Having dinner with the director?"

"I don't think there are any laws against it. It's about the play, right? If he comes on to you, we'll have him up on charges—unless of course you enjoy it. Seriously, it's not a great idea, in general, to mix those things up. But you know that."

"Oh definitely."

Then she speed dials her mother in Stamford. "Hi Mom. I got the part."

"Really?" says her mother, letting her know how surprised she is.

"Yeah, really. They actually hired me."

"No, I didn't mean it that way. I just meant you'll have to tell Uncle Vincent you can't work at the bar anymore. He'll be very unhappy about this. Are you sure you're doing the right thing?"

"They gave me the part, Mom.

"You've never done anything like this before, Olive. What do you know about Russian drama?"

"I think I can do it."

"I don't know, Olive. I don't think this is such a good time for you to be away. I'm still recovering, you know. From the hip surgery. I don't get around all that well yet."

"Aunt Bertie's there."

"Thanks a lot."

"She's your sister; she loves you, Mom."

There's a silence.

"Mom?"

Still nothing.

"Don't do this to me, Mom. It's not going to work this time. I've changed. I'm not going to let you do this to me."

"Oh, you've changed! What did you do, go to your psychiatrist again? It's not so easy to change, sweetheart. Not so easy to change your spots."

"I'll call you next week, Mom."

It's nine o'clock by the time Herbie stumbles out of the bar, loads his golf clubs into the trunk and remembers that he has his cell phone off. He retrieves Olive's two messages, gives her a call but gets her voice mail. If she wants to talk to me so bad, he thinks, why did she turn her phone off? He calls Jeffrey at home.

"Hey Tiger," says Jeffrey. "There's been a lot of excitement around here today; where have you been?"

"She got the job."

"Oh, yes, but that's just the beginning of it."

"What?"

"She and the director are right now having dinner at Joe Allen, going through the script, so to speak."

"Who is this guy?"

"Sam Harding. He's just a baby, but he's had two big hits in London—in that warehouse theater, what's it called?"

"I don't know."

"And he's directing his first film in late May. He's the new hot boy. The word is he's wanted to do *Vanya* for a while. So he's working on it as far out of town as he can—and you can't get any farther than this. Then he'll probably recast it with Brits and movie stars and take it to the West End."

"Uh-huh. How's Olive?"

"Excited. And scared. She's been trying to get you all day. Where were you, on the golf course?"

"Yeah."

"Playing night golf?"

"There was a little drinking afterward."

Jeffrey sighs.

"Come on Jeffrey, don't hold back—bust my balls about my drinking."

Jeffrey sighs again, slightly more dramatically. "Leave Olive a message and then don't turn your phone off. That's rule number one in modern communication—leave your goddamn phone on. She'll be home soon."

"I'm going to back off right now. She has a director; that's who should be directing her."

"That makes sense. But give her a call."

"Yeah."

"Oh, and one other thing—Uncle Vanya?"

"Yeah?"

"You want to know who's playing it?"

"Yeah?"

"Bob Frankel."

Driving back to the golf resort he hates, Herbie's brain is spinning. Bob Frankel as Uncle Vanya is absolutely brilliant. There aren't two actors in the world right now who could play that part better. No one can mine the smallness of the human heart like Bob Frankel. He'll be a genius Vanya—envious, pathetic, whingy, yet somehow empathetic in his odd way. And always funny. Bob never misses a laugh. All of which means that Olive could be in over her head. Herbie was thinking she'd be doing it with small-time people in the sticks somewhere and could learn a little something while she gets experience. But now there's going to be some serious acting going on and she's going to have to fight to hold her own.

He takes a shower and watches CNN for a while. Then he tries her again. It's after eleven and her phone is still on voice mail. Fuck it, he thinks and turns off his phone, smokes a little dope and goes to the bar he hates. He sits at the far end, of course, nurses a martini—he doesn't feel like drinking anymore tonight. Through the smoke in the bar, he pictures Olive sitting at a back table in Joe Allen, deep in discussion about her new script with this young, hot prick from London.

CHAPTER TEN

ERBIE'S EYES POP OPEN SHORTLY AFTER DAWN AND HE knows he's not getting back to sleep. It's too quiet, he thinks. All those years listening to Annie's sound machine raining away in his ear—he hated that fucking thing. Now its absence is tragic, unsupportable. He turns on his phone and sees that there's another message from Olive and one from Candy. Olive's voice on the machine sounds plaintive and tired, like she finally came down off the high of getting the part. It's too early to call either of them so he goes looking for coffee, which he has to admit they make pretty well at this joint. Today he's got to find another place to stay—a hotel, he thinks, not a theme park. The lobby's empty but he sees a stack of local newspapers outside the front door. He pulls one from the pile and heads to the kitchen where the night porter has the coffee machine going. Herbie gets the guy to fill up a thermos, which he then carries to the empty bar. He finds himself a mug, climbs up on the stool and starts his daily ritual of crossword and caffeination. He gets so absorbed that he doesn't notice that Don, the golf pro, also couldn't sleep this morning.

"Morning, Mr. Aaron. I'm surprised you're still here. I thought you didn't like this place."

"I'm moving today."

"You mind if I join you for a second?"

He actually does mind but some instinct tells him to offer the kid a stool.

"I've been thinking about you," says the kid.

"Sexual fantasies?"

Don blushes and shakes his head. "You are the damndest person, Mr. Aaron. You always come up with the . . . I don't know . . . the *damndest things*."

"You bring it out in me, Don."

"Have you found a golf teacher yet?"

Herbie shakes his head.

"Well, I might have an idea for you."

"Oh yeah?"

"Her name is Billy Stiles. Yeah, a woman named Billy. She's a . . . terrific gal, a real straight shooter. Mac wanted to get her to head the whole school up here because he says she's the best around, but she turned him down flat. She has to do things her way, she says. And to be honest with you, I don't think she took to all the michigas in the program."

"All right, if you're gonna add this word to your vocabulary, you have to say it right: mishigas—sometimes the accent's on the last syllable, sometimes on the first—there's a subtle difference that even I don't understand. Say it."

"Mishigas."

"And the other way."

"Mishigas," he says, accenting the last syllable. "I think I like it that way better."

"Yeah, me, too."

"Anyway, here's her number. Tell her I said hi."

They shake hands and Don walks out through the empty bar. Herbie types the number into his phone and saves it. Then he pours another coffee and walks it back to his room to call Candy, who is indeed asleep. When he hears her groggy hello, he sings to her: "Rise and shine sleepy Joe; there are places to go."

"Jesus," she says. "I haven't heard that song in a really long time."

"That's how I used to get you up for school."

"Yeah, Pops, believe me I remember. Where are you?"

"South Carolina."

"Jesus."

"What's up? Tell me something I don't know."

"Wow, another phrase from my childhood. You getting senile?"

"Is Maurice there?"

"Right next to me, smiling."

"Say hi."

"He's waving to you."

"Wait a minute. Somebody's beeping me. What do I do? What button?"

"Hit flash."

"Flash? What the fuck is flash? Oh, wait a minute."

He hits a button and loses both calls. He sits there looking at the phone, considering dropping it into his coffee. Then, out of self-preservation, it rings.

"So, when were you going to call me back?" says Olive.

"How was dinner?"

"Great. We talked about the play all night. He's really smart."

"All night?"

There's a pause.

"All evening."

"So, who went to dinner? You or Yelena?"

She doesn't reply.

"Because if it was her, you probably fucked him."

"Is this in the form of a question?"

He doesn't reply.

"First of all, you're wrong about Yelena. Maybe you don't know her so well. There's a lot of show in Yelena; a lot of show and no dough, if you know what I mean. Secondly, I went to the dinner as Olive. As myself. That's the way I go everywhere."

"As yourself?"

"Yep."

"And who might that be?"

There's a pause.

"You mean who am I?"

"Yeah. Who is this person that's in my life all of a sudden? I'd like to know."

"Is this coming from a cold place, Herbie? Because I've been getting a lot of coldness from you this morning and I don't want to . . ."

"No. Not from a cold place."

She's silent for a while, thinking. He listens to her breathe and the phone connection turns intimate.

"Well I'm not who I was yesterday. Maybe that's the best answer to your question."

He just listens.

"Everything's changing—so fast I can't believe it. And once it started I can't stop it."

"Stop what?"

"Well . . . I'm a girl, a woman that . . . all my life . . ."

Herbie listens.

"I held myself back; I hid my best self, you know?"

He knows.

"But I'm not doing that anymore."

"Why is that?"

"Because I met an amazing person a few weeks ago," she says, suddenly emotional. "And she told me I couldn't do it anymore. She wouldn't let me. She told me there was no time for that."

"Ah. Annie got to you, did she?"

"Oh my God. It was the night of my life, Herbie. Every-thing changed that night. What an incredible woman she was."

He doesn't disagree.

"She saw right into you."

"What did she see?"

She sighs a big one. "That I was afraid to outshine my mom. Really terrified of that—like life and death. So I kept my head down and I did okay, but I didn't shine. And Annie told me that wasn't going to work anymore. That if I wanted to play with the big boys I had to be my whole brilliant self."

"Yeah, that sounds like Annie."

"She told me about her pirate—you know when she discov-ered her past life as a pirate? Did she ever do the pirate for you?"

"Are you kidding? I lived with that pirate. He scared the shit out of me."

"When she was telling me, she transformed into him—right there in her hospital bed. It was terrifying."

"Yeah, she could act."

"I was the captain of my own ship," imitates Olive in her pirate voice. "And wherever I chose to sail, that's where we'd sail. When I was hungry, I tore into a side of beef with my bare hands; when I was thirsty, I downed a whole keg of ale; when I was horny, I fucked whoever I wanted—right there on the deck in front of the whole crew; and when I was tired, I just lay down where I was and went to sleep. That was the best part."

"She lived it, too. That pirate was a big part of her. There aren't many women who go after what they want—and just take it. She was rare."

"I'm going to be that kind of woman. I mean I am that kind of woman."

Herbie is smiling. "Are you?"

"I'm working on it."

"But you're scared to death about starting rehearsal."

"Well . . ."

"That's all right. If you're not scared, how are you ever going to be brave? That's even true of pirates."

"Are you gonna coach me, coach?"

"Yeah. You ready? Go out today and buy a great outfit for the first rehearsal. You should walk in there feeling like a million bucks."

"Okay. Like it should look like I just tossed something on without thinking but I look great in it?"

"Perfect. If I was there I'd go with you to pick it out."

She doesn't say anything.

"Then just remember to take your time and keep your eyes open. There's an actor named Bob Frankel who's playing Uncle Vanya. He's really good. Watch him; watch what he does. Watch how he goes about it. Then watch everybody else. And you'll notice everybody's doing something different. They're all trying to find their way into the play—just like you. There's no one way."

"Okay."

"And I'm going to back off. You have a director. You like this guy, right? Let him direct you. If I try to tell you things behind his back, it'll just fuck you up. Work with him."

"I want to keep talking with you."

"Work with the director—and the other actors. That's where the play's going to come alive. Then if you have something you want to kick around—good or bad—I'm here. You know where to find me."

"Yeah, at the bar at some golf course in Myrtle fucking Beach."

"You got it. Good luck, baby."

He hangs up and thinks that he just called her baby—in that

way—and it kind of shakes him up—like his interior balance mechanism tips to a weird angle. He sits down on the bed and waits for the room to steady itself. Then the phone jingles.

"Oh shit, Candy?"

"I'm glad to see you got that flash thing down."

"Sorry."

"Who was that, Olive?"

"Yeah. How'd you know?"

"I'm having lunch with her today."

"Ah. The women's club. She's a good kid."

"She's a oner, Pops."

"You think?"

"Mom knew."

He chews on that. He still doesn't quite have his balance back.

"So, Maurice is taking me to Venice tomorrow. The one in Italy."

"Venice," he says, impressed. "Be careful. It can get very romantic."

"Yeah, that's what they say."

"In his jet?"

"Sure."

"Keep me posted."

He showers and shaves and then gets his suitcase out of the closet and starts to throw everything into it. It's eight thirty in the morning, he thinks. I've got sixteen more hours before I can go to bed again. What am I doing down here? His breath starts to get panicky, so he sits on the bed and waits it out. I'm not doing anything, he thinks. He punches in the number for the golf teacher that Don gave him.

"Billy Stiles," she answers.

"Oh, I thought I was gonna get your machine."

"You want me to hang up?"

He laughs. "My name is Herb Aaron and I got your number from Don, the teacher at St. Andrew's?"

"Don's a good kid."

"Yeah. He said you took problem students."

"He called you that?" He could hear the laugh in her voice.

"No, actually. He wanted to, but like you say, he's a good kid."

"You a problem, Mr. Aaron?"

"Yeah, I'm a problem to me."

"Ha. Aren't we all? Where you from?"

"New York."

"Ah. So you haven't played all winter and your game's rusty. You need a little rehab."

"No, rehab won't do it; I need an intervention."

"Tell you what: I'm working today but I can meet you at six this evening and we'll talk it over. How's that?"

"Good."

"You know the Fleetwood Golf Course in North Myrtle?"

"I'll find it."

"I'll be at the bar—third stool from the left, in front of a vodka stinger. You can't miss me."

Sometimes—as Blanche DuBois famously said—there's God so quickly.

He calls the pro shop and tells them to bring his clubs up to the drop-off in front of the lobby and he calls for his car—he switched to valet parking after he couldn't find the car that night in the parking lot. Then he calls for a bellman. He feels better. He's in motion again. He has an appointment—six o'clock. Jesus, I only have nine hours to go find another hotel; better get cracking.

He heads down to the ocean, where a lot of the cheap motel chains are lined up a block off the beach. The first one he tries is just fine—clean, decent bed, decent shower. And there are bars of every variety in both directions. You could trip over the bars. He checks in and takes himself for a walk, looking for that good crab cake he had back in the seventies. A good crab cake is one of the glories of American cuisine, he lectures to the ocean. A bad crab cake is a crime against nature. People look at him as he passes by but he doesn't care. Golfers and shag dancers. What makes a great crab cake, he continues, is that it should give the appearance of being only crab—nuggets of sweet, buttery, sea-salty back fin crabmeat with a shake of Old Bay seasoning mixed in for spice—and that's it. It should seem to be held together by nothing more than its own innate desire to be a perfect crab cake. Then it should be sautéed in oil with a nice dollop of lard melted in. The lard gives the oil a nice bottom. Then, just before you serve it, one more sprinkle of Old Bay on top—so that the first thing that hits your tongue wakes up your taste buds and starts your juices going. Now he's hungry. He's talked himself into lunch.

He finds a place called the Crab Shack that touts its "Famous Crab Cakes." He goes to the bar and orders two of them and a bottle of beer. His hopes are not high. The bar still smells like last night's party—that faint mélange of sweat, urine, and sandals in desperate need of odor-eaters. When the plate appears he can tell immediately that the crab cakes are an abomination. Somebody took the mixture—made with God knows what—formed it into two balls and then rolled them in store-bought bread crumbs; then they deep-fried them in old, smelly oil. He cuts one open with a fork and tries a bit. It has the texture and taste of an old, rotted-out bird's nest. He drains the beer to get the taste out of his mouth and heads back to his car. He'll go to the driving range, he thinks; hit some balls. Stay in motion, Herb. Stay in motion.

At the stroke of six, Billy Stiles is right where she said she'd be—third stool in, curled around a vodka stinger. She's a nice-looking woman, almost certainly a lesbian, in her mid-fifties. Her hair is salt and pepper, cut simply like athletes do, and her eyeglasses—blue-tinted with rectangular lenses—show some style. Her face has seen a lot of sun and has more wrinkles than it should, but they all seem to smile instead of frown, so the effect is nice.

"I thought it was you," she says shaking his hand. "I'm a big fan. I loved your show."

"Thanks."

"And I'm sorry about your loss. I was an even bigger fan of your wife."

He nods. "Let's drink to her." Herbie gets a martini—up—and tells the barman to keep shaking. He and Billy clink their glasses without a word and take each other in.

"So, Mr. Aaron. How'd you spend your day?"

"I changed hotels and then I tried to find a decent crab cake, but no luck. I thought this town knew how to do that."

"The best crab cake in Myrtle Beach—or anywhere else for that matter—is made by my sister. No contest."

"How does she make them?"

"I have no idea—I don't cook. But they taste like there's nothing in it but crab."

"And how does one get to your sister?"

"Ah." And she raises her eyebrows inscrutably.

Herbie's shoulders drop about a foot. She gets his jokes; he gets hers. She's been around but she doesn't have to tell you about it. Billy Stiles, he thinks. Okay.

"So, tell me," she says with a good smile.

"People keep saying that my practice swing and my regular swing are completely different. And the implication is that one of them is good and the other bad. And I don't have to tell you which one is which."

"Uh-huh," she says.

"So what should I do about that?"

"Tell 'em to mind their own business."

"It's some kind of fear, right? I don't trust what I've got so I have to fuck with it some way."

"Yeah," she says, sounding bored, "that's probably it." She signals the bartender for another stinger. "How 'bout we play tomorrow—you and me? Right here at Fleetwood—it's an easy track, no hills; we won't keep score; we'll just hack it around and have some fun."

"Okay."

"Then we'll talk. If I try to get into that kind of stuff before I know you, I'll just be shooting blanks, you know?"

"Okay."

"So, what else? When are we going to see you on the screen again?"

"I don't know. I think maybe I'm done with all that shit."

"C'mon, Herb, give yourself a break. You just lost your life partner. You're still in shock, no?"

"Shock is too good a word for what I'm in. But even before Annie died—I just don't have the zest for the acting anymore. It all just seems like so much crap to me."

Herbie signals the barman. They sit in silence and watch him do his work.

"So, how do I pay you? We should work out the deal, no?

"Okay. How about two hundred for the day and you pick up the expenses."

"That's fair. How's your time? Because I'd like to do this for a couple of weeks, maybe."

"That's fine; I'll book out the afternoons. This is really still off-season anyway."

"And then you'll have to tell me how to get those crab cakes."

"Whoa, Herb. One thing at a time."

CHAPTER ELEVEN

O LIVE'S OUTFIT FOR THE FIRST REHEARSAL—WELL-WORN jeans and a drop-dead top, a white V-neck Indian lacy thing that frames her face and gently hints at the rest of her body—hits all the right notes but doesn't help quiet her nerves. Some of the actors know each other and they're gabbing away, catching up. Others grab a chair at the table and start filling out Equity forms about their health insurance and pension fund. Olive is one of these, keeping her head down. Take it slow, she thinks. Just watch and wait. And don't try to give a performance in the first read-through, Herbie said. Just try to hear the play.

The producer of the theater gives a welcoming speech, the designers show the model for the set and renderings of the costumes and then everybody excuses themselves except for the actors and Sam Harding, the director. They settle themselves around a large, round table and it's time to begin.

"I'd like to start off in what may seem to be an odd way," says Sam, who has clearly put some thought into his first rehearsal clothes, as well. "We'll read the play—as usual—but I'm going to have each of you read someone else's part. Not your own."

"Oh God," moans Bob Frankel, who's slumped down in his chair to Sam's left in the circle. He has his hand on his forehead like a man with a migraine.

"Problem, Bob?" says Sam cheerfully.

"Spare me this, Sam. Please tell me you're not going to get into this kind of crap. I've got three weeks to do Uncle Vanya. Can't we just, you know, *rehearse*? Like we'll *act* and you'll *direct*?"

"No, Bob, we can't. Not until we do this first. But thanks for your input." Again, there's no rancor in Sam's voice; but the message is clear—the play is going to be rehearsed his way. "I've written all the characters names on these little bits of paper. Just pick one out the bowl and that'll be your part for today's reading." He starts around the table with the bowl. "The only catch is if you get your own character, you have to toss it back in and take another."

Bob is now sighing, making no bones about the fact that he's suffering tragically. When the bowl gets to him—Sam went the other way around the table so that Bob is last to pick—he mutters, "Nursery-school shit," and takes the last paper.

Olive feels the blood coming up in her cheeks. She can't believe this guy. Herbie had warned her that Bob was weird, but if an actor in a musical talked to the director like this, he'd be fired; he'd be out on the street in a second. This is my first rehearsal, she thinks, and this guy is making it all about him. She takes a deep breath to steady herself but her anger won't go away.

"All right, everyone," says Sam. Let's see who's reading what." Olive looks at her crinkled scrap—"Vanya."

Bob, who has picked the role of Marina, the old nanny, is now slumped even lower in his chair. His migraine has reached stage four. He's almost inaudible as he reads the lines of the first scene with no emphasis or interpretation. The other actor—reading Astrov—tries as best he can to make a scene of it, but he has an uphill climb. Then it's time for Vanya's entrance. Olive slumps down in her chair in close parody of Bob's body language. The she puts her hand on her forehead, wrinkles her brow and deliver's Vanya's first line. She's not exactly doing an imitation of Bob, but she nails his attitude—that of disdain for all the others and utter despair for himself. For a moment the rest of the cast watches in stunned silence; then some smiles appear around the table; then a giggle or two. Sam is beaming. Bob peers up from his victim posture and after a moment of surprise, smiles and shakes his head. Even he has to grudgingly admit that Olive's portrayal is right on the mark.

"Keep reading," says Sam. "Stay focused on the play."

And they proceed with Olive playing Vanya as Bob Frankel, and Bob, jostled out of his peevishness, joining the cast in a spirited reading of the play.

To say that Olive's heart is pounding is an understatement. She feels like she's soaring above the room, looking down. She has that sense of time slowing down. It's like when your car skids off the road in a snowstorm, she thinks, and you're calmly watching yourself having an accident.

At the end of the reading, Sam stands and gives a one-man ovation to the cast. "That was superb. You are superb, one and all. Thank you. And not too shabby a play, either. This Chekhov fellow knew a thing or two, eh? Now we're going to take an hour; go have some lunch, call your agents; do whatever it is actors do, and we'll meet back here at half-past two. We'll read the play again and we're going to draw names as we did the last time. You still won't be playing your own part."

"Are you trying to kill me?" Bob has his arms stretched toward heaven, but now there's a smile in his voice.

"No, Bob. I need you. But I am trying to torture you a bit. Have a lovely lunch."

As the cast is dispersing, talking about where they'll go to lunch, Bob comes over to Olive.

"That was very clever," he says.

"I don't know what got into me." She holds his gaze.

"Oh, I think you know very well what got into you. I think you're a very clever girl." There's admiration in his tone, but also there's a subtle threat. There's a "watch out who you're playing with, sweetheart" tone in his voice, which is part of Bob's charm.

As the room empties, Olive drifts over to a table along the wall where the costume renderings are lined up. There are four costumes for Yelena, which will be built from the ground up in the costume shop. Nice change, she thinks, from the rented costumes I wore in summer stock. Yelena is a clotheshorse, so her outfits are stylish. It's Russia in the late 1800s and upper-class women often got their clothes from Paris. Olive fingers the fabric swatches and she imagines how they'll feel against her skin. The costume designer took the pains to make the character drawings resemble the actor playing the part and Olive notes the way she's been perceived—elegant, beautiful and willful. I can use these drawings, she thinks. I can hold myself like this and walk with that kind of assurance—even if, inside, I feel like throwing up. Just like Yelena. She smiles. This is what I want to do, she thinks. This is what I want to be.

Herbie is completely exhausted by the time he gets back to the motel. He's been playing golf with Billy for the last three days and it's the most consistent exercise program he's been on since he was thirty. He now has an hour to shower and shave and meet Billy and her sister at the beach for dinner. The sister wants to meet him, Billy says, and if she likes him, she'll make him crab cakes. "Another fucking audition," he says out loud.

The lessons haven't really been lessons, because Billy refuses to talk about golf. "It's not time, yet," she says. "Just hit the ball to the target, no practice swings. Watch how much faster that makes the day go."

So they talk about other things—about Annie mostly. Just when he tees the ball up and he's ready to swing away, she says, "So, how'd you guys meet?" And he launches into the whole story, telling all the gory details. Billy laughs, really getting into it and that makes Herbie all the more loquacious. There's something about the way Billy asks the questions—she really wants to know—that makes him feel like talking. And the more he talks the lighter his body gets. He's been pushing all this stuff down, working overtime trying not to think about Annie, about how much he adores her, and now it's pouring out of him like champagne from a bottle that got shaken up. There's a bit more pep in his step as he walks to his ball—yes, he's walking most of the way because Billy only rented one cart and she's in the driver's seat, so to speak. As soon as Herbie hits the ball, she drives off and tells him she'll meet him up at his next shot.

"Did you know right away that she was the one?" asks Billy as she hands him his five-iron, and Herbie tells her about the party a few weeks after they met. Annie's sitting on the kitchen floor; she's hasn't yet hit her twenty-third birthday; she has on a miniskirt with those unbelievable legs tucked under with the skirt riding up and Herbie can't keep his tongue in his mouth. Billy laughs, Herbie smiles as he unthinkingly smacks the ball and then she drives away, leaving him to walk to his next shot. And so it goes. Billy doesn't teach him at all, but he can't help but watch her game, which is simple and dazzlingly effective. She looks at the ball; then she looks at the target; then she hits the one to the other. That's it. Today is their third day and Herbie's feeling it in muscles he forgot he had, but the feeling is good.

He checks his messages and there's a long one from Olive, all about her first rehearsal and Sam's idea for the reading and the whammy she pulled on Bob Frankel. Herbie is so excited he can barely punch the numbers in.

"This is brilliant," he says when she answers the phone. "You are absolutely the pirate!"

"Yep," she says with pride.

"Bob must have shit a pickle."

Olive just smiles.

"What made you do it? Have you ever done anything like that before?"

"I was just mad. I mean I think Sam's idea for the rehearsal was great and then Bob tried to make it all about himself."

"Sam's idea was brilliant. Absolutely brilliant! What better way to keep the actors from crawling up their own assholes during the first read-through?"

"Hey, you're in a good mood."

He stops and realizes that he is. "Yeah, well, my job is done. My protégé is ready to be on her own, obviously. You're a pirate, baby. Go forth and piratize. You have a good director; you're playing the right part. Just go and do it."

"Oh, so you're in a good mood because you're done with me?"

"Yeah, thank God. I thought that was never gonna end."

"Fuck you."

Herbie smiles. "Now all you have to do is act."

"Oh yeah. So how does that go again?"

"Acting?"

"Uh-huh."

"I don't know. Either you can do it or you can't. I mean there are tricks you can learn—good tricks, like how to stay focused and how to stay out of your head and how to be present.

And simple shit like how not to upstage yourself. But either you can act or you can't; nobody can teach you."

"So can I?"

"Yeah. I'm sure of it."

"How do you know?"

"First of all, this very smart director—*very* smart, it seems to me—picked you to play the role. Now obviously he's got a hard-on for you, unless he's gay . . ."

"He's not gay."

"Okay, we got that cleared up." He pauses. "Where was I?"

"Are you stoned?"

"A little."

Olive lets out a small impatient sigh. "You were telling me why you're so sure I can act."

"Right. So the smart director cast you—that's one. And no matter how much he wants to have sex with you he's not going to cast a bad actress in his play."

"And?"

"And Annie said you could. She told me flat out. And Annie could tell a real actor at a hundred paces."

"She did?" Her voice is suddenly fourteen years old and quavering.

"Why does that make you cry?"

"I don't know. She makes me emotional."

Join the club.

Olive doesn't want to let him go. She's alone, too—in a cheaply furnished studio apartment near the theater. She's about to put a Lean Cuisine into the microwave and then curl up with her script.

"Say another really smart thing, okay?"

"Why?"

"It makes me all tingly inside."

He actually laughs. "I have to go."

"Where?"

"I'm having dinner with my golf teacher and her sister."

"Oh, the golf teacher's sister. That's why you're in such a good mood."

"I haven't even met her."

"Uh-huh. So you're done with me? No more smart things for me?"

"Okay. You know when you have to go to the hardware store to get a key made, but it's the key to the elevator, which you need to get down to the basement?"

"Yeah?"

Well, if you don't tell the guy that it's an elevator key—which is some kind of secret-code key—then the key he makes you won't work in the elevator."

"That's the smart thing?"

"That's a good piece of information."

"C'mon."

"About acting?"

"Yeah."

He thinks for a minute. "Don't let some guy—some old guy who just wants to show off his stuff—tell you how to do your job."

There's a pause.

"Big tingle."

"Talk to you tomorrow."

Billy and her sister have already corralled the curve of the bar, so that they can both sit on one side and face Herbie on the other. Very thoughtful, he thinks. The sister is kind of cute. A few years younger than Billy, she's wearing one of those long

print dresses—Laura Ashley is the name that springs to mind—
that's flattering but discreet about the shape of her body. It's just
like those quasi-hippie dresses from the seventies, very colorful,
very feminine. She has a cute, bouncy kind of haircut with wispy
bangs coming down. And she has freckles.

"Herbie, this is my sister, Roxanne."

They shake hands and Herbie sits on his stool, facing them.
"Nice to meet you," he says.

She nods and lifts her eyebrows a little as if to say maybe it
is and maybe it isn't.

"I used to watch you on TV," she says with a nice Southern
lilt.

He nods, modestly.

"You were good," she adds.

"That's it? I was good and that's it?"

"Well you were also kind of sexy, if you want to know."

"That was acting."

They smile at each other and nod a couple of times. "Okay,"
she says, "you're okay." And she digs into her purse and pulls
out a baggie with a crab cake in it. She hands it across the bar to
Herbie.

"You carry a crab cake in your purse?"

"You never know."

Billy signals the bartender and asks him for a plate and a
fork. Roxanne tells him to also bring some Worcestershire
sauce, which gets Herbie's attention. This girl knows her way
around a crab cake.

"I can't wait for you to taste it," says Billy, gently freeing the
cake from the baggie and arranging it in the center of the plate.

"I don't have to taste it. I can see from here it's a good crab
cake."

"You have to taste it," says Roxanne.

He puts a scant drop of Worcestershire onto the lower left quadrant of the cake and then forks the whole section into his mouth.

"He takes a healthy bite," notes Roxanne to Billy.

Herbie takes his time, chewing, savoring; savoring, chewing.

"This is a perfect fucking crab cake. Pardon my language."

"No offense taken. I'm glad you like it. They're better hot, right out of the fat." The thought of which makes Herbie hungry—really hungry—for maybe the first time since Annie died.

"If you want," says Roxanne, "y'all can come back to my house. I've got them all made up and ready to fry. I have salad."

"You got booze?"

"Please."

CHAPTER TWELVE

ᏕᎧ

T HE THREE OF THEM LEAVE THE BAR IN TANDEM, ROX-
anne's car in the lead, Herbie following and Billy in the
rear, making sure he doesn't stray off course.

"They've got me and they're not going to lose me," he mutters. He finds a way to load his pipe and he takes a hit when they
stop for a light. After ten minutes they're driving through an
upscale neighborhood with houses partially hidden behind stone
walls. Roxanne turns into a gated driveway that opens automat-
ically and Herbie and Billy follow her up a little hill through a
stand of manicured grounds to a contemporary-style house with
big windows looking out in all directions.

"Nice," says Herbie, as he gets out of his car.

"From upstairs you can see the ocean," says Roxanne.

"I've seen it."

Roxanne thinks this is the funniest thing she ever heard. She
takes Herbie by the arm and ushers him into the house and right
to the bar in the den.

"There's ice in that little fridge; you can bartend," she says and
goes off into the kitchen. Herbie looks at Billy and raises his eyes.

"Yeah," she says, "it's quite a place. Rox and her ex are both
big-time dermatologists and when they practiced together they
were printing money. Then he ran off with the anesthesiologist."

"To ease the pain. How long's he been gone?"

"Couple of years. He was never a good man—always on the hustle, looking out for number one. This house gives me the creeps, if you want to know the truth."

Herbie can see how uncomfortable Billy is. She seems smaller and less sure of herself in this place—suddenly like a little girl dressed up in man's clothes. Herbie does the drinks and they drift into the kitchen in time to see Roxanne drop a few cakes into the hot oil.

"So, what? You're rattling around in this place?" They're sitting on stools around the big granite island. Billy throws out a pile of forks, some napkins and plates. Roxanne turns the crab cakes and puts out some sliced tomatoes and a salad, to go along.

"I am now. Both my boys are up and out—the oldest is in med school at Johns Hopkins and my youngest is a bum."

"Where does he do that?"

"On a beach off the coast of Spain."

"Nice."

"He's a good boy for a bum." She puts the finished cakes on some paper towels to let them drain off the excess oil and then serves them up. Herbie tucks in like he hasn't eaten for a month.

"And your husband split for another woman?"

"For as many other women as he can fit in before he dies. He's on a quest."

"Well . . . I don't know if you're looking for another way to look at this, but . . . guys chase." He shrugs. "I'm not saying it's right, but the male of the species—in order to propagate the species—seems to have that in the DNA."

"Oh, DNA my ass." says Roxanne. "That's so cheap. You've got a brain, *use* it. Use your big, human brain to tell your tiny little DNA to keep your big dick in your shorts. That's all you gotta do."

Herbie's on very shaky ground, but he's had enough to drink to argue the point. "We do that—most of us—we control our urges, but that doesn't mean the urges aren't there."

"Oh Jesus, we got another one." She turns to Billy. "Why are you sitting there smirking? You think you're above all this just because you're a lesbian. You know what they say, Herbie—what does a lesbian bring to the first date? A U-Haul."

"No. I'm not above anything," says Billy amiably. "I just think the two of you are so adorable I can't stand it."

"Oh fuck you, Billy."

The three of them suddenly realize just how loaded Roxanne has gotten herself. Billy stretches out her hand across the island and touches her sister on the arm—a soft caress with her fingers, like you might do on a little kitten.

"I gotta go, tiger. Work in the morning."

"I'm sorry, Billy. I didn't mean to say fuck you."

"I probably deserved it; don't worry about it. See you tomorrow, Herb. You know your way out of here."

"Yeah, I'm fine."

"Now, don't think you have to go prove your point or anything—you know, about how men just have to be men and all."

"I'll see you tomorrow. Same time."

"Same time."

Roxanne blows her a kiss and then pours herself a glass of bubbly water. She starts to clear the table and Herbie pitches in.

"I got drunk," she says. "I think I was nervous."

"Why?"

"I don't know. You're famous and Billy thinks the world of you. And I haven't been seeing many men. I'm still too pissed off, as you can see. But don't get me wrong; I'm not looking for anything to happen here. You're off the hook."

"No, I'm not ready for that anyway. I can't . . . think about that right now. It's too confusing."

"I get it. So we'll talk a bit. You want coffee?"

"No, keeps me up."

"Some people can drink it and go right to sleep. Not me, either."

Herbie goes to the bar and tops up his drink. Then he comes back to the granite island. "So what was good about your husband when you liked him?"

She sighs. "Ted's real good-looking and he's a smart man. And a fine doctor, a good scientist. But as a human being, he was and always will be a piece of shit. And the more successful he got as a doctor, the more he thought he was God. And once you know you're God, well . . . you're not going to be listening to your wife telling you what to do, are you?"

Herbie puts his head down and tightens his lips, in that way he has. "What if you were God, too?"

"I'm sorry?"

"Roxanne, we all think we're God. It's just that some people admit it and some people don't."

She looks at him like he's crazy.

"Okay, let me use another word because 'God' freaks people out. I mean we all look at life like we're at the center, looking out—it's all happening around us—to us—right?"

"Okay, I get that."

"But there are some people who think, no it's not happening *to* me, it's happening *for* me—this show is put on for *me*—for *my* amusement, for *my* pleasure—and I can go this way or I can go that; I have a menu—I can chose to do—or have, or be—whatever I want. We all want to be that way but most of us don't have the balls."

"I'm sorry, Herbie, I've had a lot to drink and I'm a little foggy, but it sounds to me like you're going into this deep, philosophical . . . thing—just so that you can justify the fact that you liked to chase pussy while you were married."

He thinks for a minute. "Maybe."

They clink glasses and smile.

"That's all you're going to say? About being God?"

"Well, now you got me thinking about pussy."

"Ha!"

"Tell me about Billy."

"Billy is my big sister. She is my knight in shining armor. She is the finest human being on God's earth. What else you want to know?"

"Does she have someone?"

"She did. Marianne. They were together for a long time— longer than my marriage lasted. She died a little over a year ago. Of breast cancer—same as your wife."

This news takes Herbie all the way down. Whatever crag he has crawled himself out of—so as to feel and talk and breathe like a human being again—crumbles under the weight of this news. Death, aloneness; Billy and her dead partner; Annie gone forever; the whole mishigas. He sits there unable to think of anything to say. Roxanne's at a loss, too. She knows she sank him and there's no way back from that. Finally she pokes him, fairly sharply in the arm. "So, you still like to chase girls?"

It was the right thing to say. "No, I got too old for that. But occasionally I let 'em chase me."

And they have a good laugh over that.

Herbie feels good when he gets back to the motel. Roxanne is fun. She's good for him to be around. When he left, he asked her out for dinner the next night. He said he'd take her for a steak and she said fine.

He checks his phone and there's a message from Olive. "Call me no matter how late. I want to hear about the golf pro's sister." There's a smirk in her voice that bothers him. He sits on the bed and thinks about why he's irked. Is Olive really jealous or is this all just a tease? To make an old guy feel better when he's down. A pity tease. That's got to be what it is, he decides, and he's not feeling up to that at the moment. A pity tease makes an old guy feel worse, not better. If she were a little older she'd know that. I didn't get anything like that from Roxanne, he thinks—no false moves, no bullshit flirting. He's now got himself worked up into a snit about Olive and he turns his phone off for the night. Let her think about it.

In bed his mind is racing. The dope hasn't worn off yet and his mind's eye is stuck on an image he has of Olive when he saw her at the memorial service, in that simple dress, with her sad mouth, in that ethereal light that seemed to come from nowhere. Where the fuck was that light coming from?

CHAPTER THIRTEEN

❧

THE NEXT MORNING OLIVE TRIES HERBIE AGAIN AND his phone is still off. She leaves another message. "Hey you. Are you mad at me? Did you elope with that woman? I have rehearsal at eleven, so call me back before then if you get this. I think we start to stage the play today, which is pretty exciting, but I need you to tell me some more smart things—like don't trip over your feet and other insights like that. Call me, okay?"

Olive is feeling agitated. She's pretty sure Herbie didn't call her back deliberately. She paces the floor of the tiny apartment trying to remember what she said the night before until she decides to put her coat on and take a walk. She puts her script into her handbag so that she can go straight to rehearsal at eleven.

It's cold outside and that's good. She puts her hands in her pockets and sets a brisk pace going nowhere in particular. She passes the theater and sees the poster for the play with her name in alphabetical order with the rest of the cast. Even that doesn't make her feel better. She picks up her pace. I don't know what I'm so upset about, she thinks. He'll call when he calls. I've got my rehearsal and that's what I have to concentrate on. I mean, my God, it's not like I need Herbie to do this play. I have a director to guide me along when I need help, wonderful actors to work with; I don't need to talk to Herbie about every damn thing that comes up. Then, as if he heard that, her phone rings.

"Hey, where you been?"

"Sleeping it off," he says.

"Late night?"

"I guess so."

"Are you mad at me?"

"I was a little bit."

"Because I teased you about the golf pro's sister?"

"She has a name."

"Oh. Sorry. What's her name?"

"Roxanne."

"Nice."

"You sound like I killed your dog. What's going on, Olive?"

"Nothing. I mean if you liked her, that's great. If you've got a thing for her, I'm okay with that."

"I don't have a thing. But let's say for a minute I did. Is that a problem for you?"

She feels tears coming up, so yeah, she thinks, it's a problem.

"What's she like?"

He sighs.

"I'm serious. I really want to know. Is she good-looking? Is she a babe?"

"You know you're talking like a sixteen-year-old kid?"

"I'll tell you what, don't give me any more shit about how young I am. Because it's insulting."

"I'm lost here, Olive. What do you want?"

"I'm late for rehearsal."

"No, tell me. What do you want from me?"

"I don't know; maybe nothing." She starts to walk but she can't lose the lump in her throat. "Just don't disappear on me like that, okay? Don't do that. I gotta go." And she disconnects.

When she gets to the rehearsal studio, the rest of the cast has already started to gather around the big table. She apologizes to Sam for being late and he tells her she's not, she's fine. Just take a minute, he says. Get yourself together and then we'll start another read-through.

"I thought we were getting on our feet today."

"No, not yet. No hurry, is there?" And he holds her eye a little longer than need be, just to let her know that he likes looking at her. Olive takes it in, just to let him know that she doesn't mind.

"We're going to read again," says Sam to the cast. "Actually we're going to read for the rest of the week. But if anyone feels an undeniable urge to get up, walk around or change seats so that you can be next to the person you're doing the scene with, feel free."

"Ah," says Bob. "You want us to stage the play for you."

"Precisely. Shall we?"

And they begin to read the play. Some of the actors stay bolted to their chairs, not ready to commit to movement; others shift their chairs to different places around the table; some stand while they're playing a scene only to sit again when their characters are offstage. Alvin McConnell, who plays Astrov, decides to pace around the table whenever he's talking. Bob joins him during one of their scenes together and the company laughs as the two actors circle the room, philosophizing all the way.

Sam is delighted. When they get through the play, he calls a lunch break and says that when they get back, they'll spend the afternoon doing the same thing again. Olive crosses over to Bob, who's getting his coat on.

"Hi Bob."

"Hello, pretty one."

Olive freezes. She has something to ask him, but she doesn't quite know how to begin. Bob stares at her—and when he stares, his eyes fairly pop out of his head. It's like talking to an angry lizard.

"So," he says, "Do you hate our director? Is he driving you as crazy as he is me?"

"No, I think he's great," she says.

"Well, he's clever, I'll give you that. All you young people are very clever."

"What are you doing for lunch?" she asks.

Bob looks at her like she has two heads. "You want to have lunch with *me*?"

Olive laughs. "If you don't mind."

"I don't have lunch in the actual sense of word. I get some soup from the health-food store and find a bench in the park and I try not to freeze to death."

"Sounds like fun. May I join you?"

"It's a public park."

Olive gets her coat on and they set off to the health-food store. Bob wears a Russian fur hat that covers the bald part of his head and the curly, gray fringe sticks out around his ears and down his neck, in dire need of a haircut. He sets a brisk pace and Olive has to scamper to keep up with him. Finally, she gets up her courage and taps him on the shoulder. He stops abruptly and looks at her as if she's attacked him.

"What?"

"You know Herbie Aaron, don't you?"

Bob is surprised. "Of course I know him. He's my closest friend."

Olive tries to stifle a grin.

"You think that's funny. Why? Did he tell you something nasty about me?" He shakes his head in disgust. "That doesn't bother me; he's still my best friend. We both loved the same woman and that can make you very close. You know Herbie? How could I not know that you know him?"

"I just met him recently and I . . ."

"You know that his wife died?"

"Yes. I met Annie, as well—the week before she died."

Bob's face is a mask of pain. He can't speak.

"Maybe we should keep walking," says Olive after a moment. "We don't have that much time."

"I can't do that."

"I'm sorry?"

"Walk and talk at the same time. I don't do that. I either forget what I'm saying or I stumble. I walk or I talk."

"I just saw you do it in rehearsal. When you walked around the table with Alvin."

Bob thinks about it for a moment. "That wasn't me. That was Vanya. He apparently has no trouble with it."

"Well, maybe we'd better get our soup first and then we can talk."

"Suit yourself." They walk for a few more paces and then Bob wheels on her. "What do you mean you met Annie? You were in the hospital? Did Herbie take you there?"

"She asked him to bring me. She wanted to talk with me about him."

"A stranger? She wanted to talk with a stranger?"

"Yes; I think because . . ."

"What did she say? Did she say anything about me?"

"No."

"Then why are you bringing this up? This is painful for me. I didn't see her in the end. I couldn't. And you were with her? You talked to her? This is incomprehensible to me."

Bob starts to walk again, leaving Olive to catch up.

"I want to ask you about Herbie," she says when she catches him.

Bob stops. Olive has never seen anyone in such pain.

"I loved her like no one has ever loved anyone. You can't have any idea how strong this love was. I'm still possessed by it. But I could never talk to her; I got all flustered. I couldn't even look at her when we were in the same room. The emotion was too strong."

He starts to walk again. Then he turns and charges back to her.

"The only person who understood me was Herbie. He loved her, too, so he understood. And because he loves me, he would let me talk to him about it. He helped me to live with it. Herbie is very important to me. My entire adult life, he's the only person I can really talk to and . . . and not have to pretend I'm not who I am. Do you understand what I'm talking about? Herbie is rare."

Olive nods and gently takes his arm. "Let's get our soup."

"Right." Bob is still shaken and he allows Olive to walk with him, arm-in-arm to the health store, where they get their soups and pay for them in silence. Then they start for the park. Suddenly, Bob stops and looks at her with an uncomprehending look.

"He picked you up in a bar? While Annie was dying?"

"Not like that."

"Jesus. He's unbelievable. What is it with him? He's catnip to women. Can you explain this to me?"

"You just explained it to me."

Olive guides him to the bench, gently helps him take the lid off his soup and hands him a plastic spoon. "The soup is getting cold," she says.

"What are you, the caterer?"

* * *

When they get back to rehearsal, Sam waves to Olive from the stage manager's table across the room. She waves back, a bit puzzled and he gestures for her to come over.

"What, Sam? Am I fired?"

"Hardly. I was wondering if you'd like to have dinner together tonight."

"Sam . . ."

"I'm not making a move. I promise. I can't; I'm your director; that would be heinous and I'd be banished from working in America forever. But I can throw together a little pan-seared salmon with vegetables; we'll have a little wine and feel like human beings in this strange remote outpost we find ourselves in. Seriously, no come-on, clean and chaste, all aboveboard. What do you say?"

She pauses. "I guess so. Sure, why not." She smiles, a little ruefully at him and takes her place at the table. She really doesn't want to start anything with Sam. She's confused enough already. The reading starts and when they get to Olive's first scene, she finds herself speaking in a tiny voice, unable to get herself behind the words. She feels Sam's eyes on her and she's self-conscious. Fuck this, she thinks. If he were a good director, he wouldn't do this to me just before I rehearse; it's like he's inserting himself between me and the work. Herbie knows about this, she thinks. Herbie knew to pull away when I started working. He lived with an actress for all those years; he knows. She feels an overwhelming desire to talk to him.

During her second scene, she notices Bob looking over at her, his forehead all wrinkled and his eyes popping out. He knows something's off, she thinks, and he's worried for me. On an impulse, she gets up from her chair, crosses around the table and sits next to him. They don't have a scene together at this point, so there's no sense to it, but she sits down next to Bob and immediately manages to get herself more focused on the play. Bob is the anti-Sam, she thinks with a smile.

After the rehearsal, Bob comes up to her. "What happened there? You lost your focus. Was it me? Did I upset you during lunch? I have a way of doing that to people; it's a gift I have."

"No, it wasn't you."

"It wasn't me? Then what? I'm curious."

"Sam asked me to have dinner with him tonight and for some reason that threw me off."

"Oh, sex. It's everywhere, isn't it? It's all around me, all the time and I never see it. Listen," he takes her by the arm like a Dutch uncle, "there's plenty of time for that after we open. Tell him to buzz off."

Sam is tripping over himself to apologize; he realized his mistake the moment Olive opened her mouth in rehearsal. "Darling, please forgive me. I was being a perfect asshole." He pronounces it in the British way—ahhhshole—and that makes her smile.

"I was pretty awful in the reading wasn't I?"

"Oh my God, no. You're incapable of being anything other than wonderful. But I'll pull back; I'll let you do your work. No dinners, no flirtations; just business, okay?"

"Thanks."

"And then, once the whole thing is over, all rules are off."

He grins and she shakes her head and waves good-bye. When she gets back to her apartment, she calls Herbie and miraculously his phone is on and he answers it.

"You still mad?"

"I wasn't mad."

"Then what?"

"I can't quite figure out what you're looking for here. Sometimes you talk to me like I'm your lover, which we both know

I'm not and that throws me off. It's like I'm in a show and I don't know what part I'm supposed to play. I mean if you're working out your father issues, you're talking to the wrong guy. Just ask my daughter. I'm lousy at that job."

"So was my dad."

"I can't help you with that. Get a shrink."

"What if I do have father issues and they have nothing to do with you? Have you ever thought of that? Maybe my relationship with you is one thing and my father issues are another thing altogether. Isn't that possible?"

"No, not possible. I'm old, I've been around, I'm smart—so you want to make me into the good father. But I don't want the part. Kindly old Geppetto. I don't see myself that way."

"What part do you want to play?"

He thinks for a moment. "I'll play the confused guy. I play that part very well."

That makes her laugh. "I think we're still trying to figure out what we are to each other. I mean we haven't known each other all that long, right?"

"Right."

"I just know that you felt far away from me today and I didn't like it. Can I say that? Does that confuse you?"

"No."

Then she tells him all about her lunch with Bob and then about how Sam came on to her and about how bad her acting was after that. She goes on and on, the whole story spilling out of her, feeling so happy to be talking to him again.

"He really threw you off, huh?"

"It just felt weird, you know?"

"Maybe it felt weird because you really wanted to go to his apartment and see what pops up."

"Come on, Herbie."

"Why not? He's an attractive guy; you're out of town, all alone; you're in the prime of your womanhood. Why wouldn't you want to fuck him? It'd be a great way to release some tension, no?"

"Because I don't, that's all."

There's a silence.

"Are you going out tonight with what's her name?"

"Roxanne. Yeah, I'm taking her for a steak."

"Ah."

"It's not like that. Her husband left her for an anesthesiologist and she's feeling low. She's sad; I'm sad; it's a bond. If there was anything more to it, I wouldn't be going out with her."

"Why?"

"Because my heart has been shanghaied by a mysterious young beauty who toys with it like a tiddledywink."

"A what?"

"That's a toy we used to play with back in the fifties—a little plastic disc that you flicked with another plastic disc into a glass. The guy that gets the most into the glass wins."

"I don't think your heart is a tittlydink."

"Yeah, you do. Just an old toy that you'll play with 'til you're bored and then you'll go off and play with kids your own age."

"That's really unfair, Herbie. You don't know me well enough to say that."

Herbie conjures an image that's been on his mind a lot. He's in a room with her and it's time to take off his clothes. His skin is sagging in places where there used to be muscle tone. His drinker's belly protrudes over the waistband of his underpants. He looks in her eyes and sees what she sees.

"I'll call you tomorrow," he says and disconnects.

CHAPTER FOURTEEN

⁓

ERBIE'S DAILY SESSIONS WITH BILLY STILL DON'T really have much to do with golf. Sometimes, if he's in the middle of telling her a story, he'll just kick his golf ball further up the fairway so as not to disrupt his train of thought. He tells her more about Annie, about all the adventures of their life together—how they went from poor to rich and then back to something in between, from being nobodies to big celebs and then back to that gray area of "Hey, weren't you that guy?" None of that shit mattered, he tells Billy. All that mattered was that were alive and in the game and crazy about each other. Nobody had what we had. Billy just listens, nods her head and hits her perfect golf shots.

He talks about how they loved to live outside the rules, like they had a magic passport that allowed them to travel back and forth between different worlds and different cultures. One night they'd be hobnobbing with billionaires on Park Avenue and the next they'd be eating Chinese take-out in some artist's loft in Lower Manhattan. They sucked all the fun out whatever situation they were in—they didn't give a damn what side of the fence they were on.

We never duplicated each other, he tells her. We let our distinct personalities stay distinct. Annie was a self-improver, a seeker, whereas I was a sloth, born and bred. She would spend hours in the morning doing her yoga and meditation, standing on her head, chanting some shit or other. Then she'd eat her yogurt and granola, down her health supplements and she'd be off to her singing lesson, her Pilates class or whatever. I would just sit there like a lump on my kitchen stool with my coffee, doing the crossword puzzle. She was all motion; I was all stasis. She was health food and vitamins; I was fat and salt. And booze. And here I am alive and she's gone. What the fuck sense is there, he asks Billy. Where's the fucking sense to it? And he smacks his drive into the lake. Billy tosses him another ball and tells him to hit it harder.

Some days he just trudges up the fairway in silence, head down, ruminating on something or other and Billy lets him be. Other times, she prods him. "So what are you gonna do now? What's your next move?"

"I'm fucked, Billy. I can't go this way and I can't go that way."

"What's that about?"

"On the one hand I can't not be with a woman; I've lived too long in the company of a woman to try to remake myself and go it alone; but to go for somebody else I have to let go of Annie and that scares the shit out of me."

"Why?"

"Being with Annie, having her on my arm when I walked into a room, created a personality—or completed a personality—that wasn't there before I was with her. Yeah, completed is it. I used to be partly me and then I was all of me, you understand? My identity, my persona, was completed when I was with her. If I let her go, then what's left of me is gonna be like . . . Pee Wee Herman or something."

"Oh Jesus Christ."

"Well, you asked."

Another day she asks about his kids and he tells her about

Candy, about how terrific she is, about how everyone in the world thinks she's fantastic except her. "Like she has this little kink or a chink, you know?"

"What's she got, a kink or a chink?"

"Like a chink in her armor, you know? An Achilles chink. I think it's because she was Annie's daughter. When she looked at her mother and how fantastic she was, she lost confidence in herself in comparison. Even though the rest of the world sees her as fantastic, she can't see it."

"Give her time."

Herbie shakes his head. "No, she's had plenty of time, believe me. She's got a chink."

"Now you sound like a father," and she shakes her head grimly.

"Oh," says Herbie, and he stops in the middle of the fairway and looks at Billy. "You got a father problem?"

"Not anymore."

"Now he understands you?"

"Now he's dead."

"That doesn't solve anything. Believe me, death doesn't solve shit. So what? He had trouble that you were gay?"

"No, I was gay from the get-go; he had plenty of time to get used to that. He was just a father, you know? I was never quite what he wanted me to be. He always expected something more—better grades when I was in school; bigger college with a nationally ranked golf team; then he wanted me to go on the LPGA Tour, thought I could be a big star. Never occurred to him that's not what I wanted for myself. You fathers have to realize that we don't live our lives to get you off the hook. We want to live for ourselves—just like you do."

Herbie gets silent again for a while. He actually starts to concentrate on hitting the golf ball for a change. After a few holes of that, he plops himself down in the golf cart next to Billy. "If your father was here right now I would tell him that you're plenty good enough."

On the eighteenth fairway Billy brings up Roxanne—not in any pushy way, just to take a reading on how Herbie reacts. He clams up again and puts a big frown on his face.

"Hey, I don't mean to put you on the spot; I was just wondering if you guys are having a nice time together."

"Yeah, we're having a nice time. She's a fun woman—fun to be with, but I don't want to get her thinking that this is going somewhere. It wouldn't be fair."

"You're not ready yet. She knows that."

He doesn't say anything for a while. Billy is not a person he wants to lie to.

"There's this other woman. And I'm having trouble getting her out of my mind. That's one of the reasons I came down here."

"What's wrong with her?"

"Too young."

"Ah."

They get to the eighteenth green and Billy deftly putts out. "So you have one woman you don't want and another woman you're afraid to want."

"Yeah. And one woman that's dead."

He lines up a three-foot putt and knocks it six feet past the hole.

"You've got be the worst putter I've ever seen," says Billy.

"I hate this fucking game." He kicks the ball into the sand trap and walks off the green.

An hour later, they're at the bar, still deep in conversation. Billy is telling him about her life with Marianne, about how they were the straightest couple in the neighborhood.

"We were the opposite of you and Annie. All we wanted to do was fit in and be good citizens and not have anybody look at us funny, you know? We were the straightest lesbians in the history of the world. It was pathetic."

"What did she do?"

"We both taught at the college; that's where we met. Mari was an intellectual. The real McCoy. She wrote books; scholarly stuff. Eighteenth-century French literature was her field. Ain't that a kick that she wanted to be with me?"

He smiles at her.

"I'm a jock, that's all I am."

"You're a monster, Billy. She was lucky to find you."

She looks morose for a minute; then she brightens up and raises her glass. "Here's to love," she says and they clink.

Herbie signals the barman to shake up another martini.

"Here's what I want to know," he says.

"Shoot."

"How come you, a little squit of a thing—I've got to have forty pounds on you, right? How come you hit every shot thirty yards farther than I do?"

"Ah. Finally comes the question of length, the great male obsession. What took you so long?" She takes her glasses off and cleans them with a napkin. Then she puts them back on and peers at him with an ironic smile. "Maybe you're not swinging hard enough yet."

"I know you don't mean that."

"No, I don't. C'mon, let's go to the range. It's time for you to learn something."

"It's dark out."

"I'll protect you."

They decide to take Herbie's car because he's got his clubs in the trunk. But Billy says she'll drive because she knows the way. As they're walking across the parking lot, Billy's got her hands in her pockets and her eyes focused on the asphalt.

"You're in love with your swing, right."

"Yeah, don't change my swing."

"Okeydoke."

"Why? What's wrong with it?"

"You ever watch Ernie Els? Or Vijay Singh?"

"Yeah," he says, getting nervous.

"You notice how those swings look like warmed-up honey, no effort at all, no rush? They're in perfect balance, in perfect tempo?"

"Yeah. And what's my swing look like?"

She starts the car, drives out of the lot and turns right. "You ever see that video where the hunters are clubbing those baby seals to death?"

They drive in silence while Herbie chews on that one. She gets onto the service road that parallels the interstate and heads south. Then she pulls into the parking lot of a dilapidated driving range that looks like it's been closed for years. Herbie gets his clubs from the trunk and Billy goes around to the side of a little shack and lets herself in with a key. A minute later, the lights on the range come up. She brings out a big bucket of beat-up balls and sets them next to an Astroturf driving mat with one of those rubber golf tees sticking up through it. She places a ball on the tee.

"Hit away."

And Herbie takes the driver and starts to hit. Billy keeps putting the next ball on the tee and calling out the distance of his last shot.

"One ninety."

"One ninety? You gotta be kidding. These balls are no good. I hit it better than one ninety, for Christ's sake."

He puts a little more into the next one. Billy tees up another ball. "Two hundred. Maybe two oh five with the roll."

"Fuck you," says Herbie, and tears into the next one.

"One eighty-five."

"These balls are dead. This is ridiculous."

Billy takes the club from him and effortlessly strokes the ball.

"How far?" she asks.

"Two forty," he says, squinting into the lights. "Well, past two forty."

"You're right. The balls are dead."

Herbie grabs the club and grimly starts whaling away, barely waiting for Billy to set the next ball up. He breaks a sweat, although the evening is cool. Billy just tees the balls up, saying nothing now, and the harder he swings the more pathetic the flight of the ball is. But that doesn't stop him from swinging even harder. When all the balls are gone, he keeps swinging, now trying to smash the rubber tee through the mat and into the ground. Finally the head breaks off the shaft of the club and goes bouncing into the darkness. He stands there, breathing heavy, drenched in sweat.

"Who you trying to kill, slugger? Mama or Papa?"

Herbie just stares at her and then tosses the broken club away.

"All right. First, here's what you should do about your golf game: take two weeks off. Then quit."

"That's an old joke."

"Yeah, but it works in your case. Once golf is no longer about killing your mother with a stick, it'll lose all its interest for you; you'll find it dumb. It has way too many Republicans hanging around anyway, with funny-colored pants on."

"You got that part right."

"Okay, that's done. Now let's learn something."

Herbie looks at her like she's about to hit him.

"You like that swing of yours because it makes you feel strong."

"Right."

"That's your ego."

"Okay."

"Which is fine if what you want is to stroke your ego, but it doesn't make the ball go very far."

He concedes that with a shrug.

"You want to be in control of all that power you feel, right?"

"Sure."

"Well, here's the deal—and you felt it tonight, so you know it's true—the more control you have, the more you limit your possibilities."

He stares at her. The lights are reflecting in her glasses so he can't see her eyes. But he knows they are steady and gray, peering at him to see if he got what she just said. He feels dizzy. He sits down on the fake grass mat and thinks about it.

"So, you're not talking about golf."

"No, fuck golf."

CHAPTER FIFTEEN

O LIVE AND THE REST OF THE CAST ARE BECOMING MORE
and more Russian as the rehearsals proceed. During the
breaks they sip hot sugary tea—from a glass, not a cup—
and yearn mournfully for Moscow. At night, when their work is
done, they collect in a dark bar near the theater, knock down shots
of Stoli and reveal to one another their deepest insecurities. This
is what happens when you rehearse a play—your world narrows
down to that particular place and the problems of those particular
people and everything else may as well be on the far side of the
moon. That's why spouses and significant others get so furious
around the third week of rehearsal—because they don't exist anymore. They live in what's called the real world, doing what people
consider to be real things while their actor spouses are brooding
away their afternoons at a Russian country estate, pretending a
couple of coat stands are a grove of poplar trees.

Bob has now ingested Uncle Vanya into his personality and
is even more obnoxious than his usual obnoxious self. Olive, who
had been having lunch with him every day, now runs in the other
direction when she sees him coming because, like Vanya, he's
taking delight in the flaws of everyone else in the company. He
even perspires in character, producing tiny drops of flop-sweat
on his forehead whenever anyone looks him directly in the eye.

Olive is wearing a rehearsal costume, which is a thrown-
together skirt made of cheap muslin that approximates the

length and weight of the costumes she'll be wearing in the show. It gives her the feel, the heft, and the motion of those late nineteenth-century fashions. It flares when she turns, revealing the tops of her high-button shoes, which pleases her no end. She has become the most outrageous flirt east of St. Petersburg and has everyone—men, women, the androgynous second-assistant stage manager—madly in love with her. Sam has failed dismally in his promise to leave her alone. He can't help himself. He tries to focus when he's giving notes to the other actors but his eyes are not in his control. His infatuation—and rejection, because Olive refuses to acknowledge his attentions—are now very public and the other actors take turns buying him shots of vodka and stroking his ego. It's all very, very Russian.

Another thing happens in the third week of rehearsal: the maniacs take over the asylum. Or rather the actors, who have been living twenty-four hours a day in the skins of their characters now know more about who they are than does the director—or the playwright for that matter if, indeed, the playwright is still alive. If the playwright is dead, it doesn't matter how much he knows.

And this shift, this change in who is holding the reins, has altered Olive's take on Sam. Whereas she used to be in awe of his intelligence, his knowledge of Russian drama, his theater savvy, his cute accent—now she looks upon him more as an earnest, well-intentioned boy—a smart boy, an adorable boy—but, alas, a boy.

Enter our hero. Herbie knows how to deal with an actress in the third week of rehearsal. He's made a lifetime of it. He knows that he must never take the wind out of her sails, that she is the captain of her pirate ship and his job is to stay below decks, bailing with a bucket. Olive calls him every night before she turns in. It's often late because the cast is at the bar long into the night, but when she gets home, she takes off her makeup, goes over her script for half an hour or so, then snuggles into bed and calls Herbie.

They talk about everything. Olive vents to him about Bob, about how impossible he's become, and Herbie tells her to use it for the play—"Yelena feels the same revulsion for Vanya as you do for Bob, so use it. At this point, your instincts are gold; nothing you do can possibly be wrong; if Bob makes you feel sick, just feel sick; it's all good."

"I miss you," she tells him in Yelena's most seductive voice. "I wish you were here."

Herbie doesn't take the bait.

"You said trust my instincts, right? My instinct is to wish that you were here."

"I'm where I'm supposed to be. You don't need any more distractions up there."

"Are you a distraction?"

"I would be."

"How's your golf?"

"My teacher told me to quit."

"Oh, honey."

"I still play every day—more just to hang with Billy. I like her a lot."

"Still seeing the sister?"

"We go out to dinner."

She nods but he can't see it. "Sam told me that the more I play Yelena, the more beautiful I get."

"He can't leave it alone, can he?"

"He's a puppy."

"Yeah, he likes to play—all those games he had you playing in the beginning of rehearsal. But playful isn't a bad thing for a director to be. Not so bad for a lover, either."

"He's a boy."

"Just add the word 'toy' and you're in business."

"Don't shove me at him, okay?"

"Okay."

"I'll manage my own sex life."

He nods but she can't see it. "Speaking of which, how's the Astrov?"

"Alvin McConnell. You know him?"

"I know who he is. Good actor, no?"

"He's great and he's a wonderful guy, but I'm having a hard time feeling sexy about him. He's kind of soft, you know? I mean I love him as a person. I love talking to him, he's funny and sweet, tells me all about his family, but, you know, Yelena has to feel some heat for him."

"She does. It's crucial."

"It's frustrating."

"This is where acting comes in."

"Yeah, but I'm kind of past pretending right now—like you said, I'm feeling what I feel."

"Annie had this problem a lot over the years."

"And?"

"She substituted; she made the guy into somebody else."

"Like who?"

"Viggo Mortensen, as I recall, worked pretty well."

"Hmm."

"You know, make him into somebody who turns you on the way Astrov turns on Yelena."

"So I should think of someone who gives me a tingle when he talks?"

Again, Herbie doesn't respond.

"So, you won't come up?"

"I'll be there for the opening. After the pressure."

A couple of nights later, Herbie's at the bar waiting for Billy and Roxanne. They're all on for lobster at the fish place they like. Herbie is sitting at a table in the bar area nursing a white wine—yeah, that's right, white wine. He's been cutting back on the drinking a bit and his pants are fitting better. The waitress brings him another wine and he starts to tell her that he hasn't finished the one he has when she points over to the bar.

"Those people just bought you a drink," she says.

He looks around and sees Candy and Maurice waving to him and smiling like two little kids. Herbie gets up and holds his arms out as if to say, where the hell did you come from? And Candy rushes over and gives him a big hug.

"We're getting married, Daddy. And you have to give the bride away." She waves her ring finger in his face.

"Holy shit, look at that thing."

"Maurice wanted to make sure I got the message."

Maurice gets a bottle of champagne and three glasses and brings it over to the table.

"Hi, Dad," he says to Herbie.

"You must never say that again," says Herbie, wagging a serious finger at him. "I don't care what, why or how, you must never use that term with me again as long as you live."

"My first father rejected me, too."

Herbie holds up a warning hand as Maurice fills the glasses with champagne and the three of them clink.

"How the hell did you find me here?"

"I have ways," says Maurice with a shrug.

"What does that mean? You had me followed? You put a tail on me?"

"Let's not get too dramatic about it. I have a guy."

"You fucking had me followed," says Herbie, getting a little steamed.

"Herbie, lighten up, all right? We wanted to surprise you. And we did. Surprise! That's all."

"What, did you fly down here in your little plane?"

"It's not so little, Pops. We came as soon as we got back from Venice. I didn't want to tell you over the phone. I wanted to see your face. But I have to tell you, your face doesn't look so good."

"I don't like the idea that I'm being followed. It's creepy. Like somebody's prying into my life."

"You don't have a life," says Maurice. "The guy says you don't do a fucking thing. You play golf, you drink, you go to sleep. What's to find out?"

"Pardon me," says Billy as she joins the group at the table. "I don't mean to butt in but I have dinner plans with this gentleman."

"You're Billy," says Candy.

"How the hell did you know that? Tell me that, if you're not following me. How'd you know she was Billy?"

"Because I'm the lesbian. That's a no-brainer. You think straight people dress like this?"

"I'm Candy. I'm the daughter." She gives Billy a hug. "And this is Maurice, my fiancé."

"Hey, wow! You got engaged! In Venice? That's terrific."

The three of them hug and Herbie just stands there taking it all in, shaking his head.

"And I'm the sister," says Roxanne as she joins the group.

"Roxanne!" says Candy.

"Yeah, that's right."

"The dermatologist!"

"Jesus Christ," says Herbie in disgust. "It's old home week."

Maurice waves to the bartender for more champagne and glasses and the party gets rolling.

"We're going for lobster," says Roxanne. "Why don't y'all join us?"

"Oh my God, she said y'all. That's so adorable," says Candy. And she toasts with Roxanne.

"Let me see that ring, sweetheart. My God. Be careful with that thing; you could kill somebody."

"Y'all's is not so bad either," says Candy, looking at Roxanne's rock.

"Yeah, but I lost the husband, so it's a little tarnished, you know?"

"I would like to make a toast," says Billy with her glass on high. She takes a long pull on the drink to wet her whistle.

"This isn't very good champagne, is it, Maurice?"

"No, Billy, it's pretty piss-poor, actually."

"Yeah, I thought you'd say that. This lobster place we're going, however, has some good French stuff. I have indulged myself on numerous occasions."

"Excellent," says Maurice, who already thinks the world of her.

"Now my toast." She raises her glass again and clears her throat. "Here's to the father of the bride. Herbie, I've only known you a couple of weeks, but you are the most fun that's come down the pike in a long time. Here's to your daughter's engagement: may Candy and Maurice always be as happy and in love as they look right at this moment."

Billy drains her glass as do the others, with ringing endorsements and "hear, hears" and all that. Herbie is standing there, realizing there's no way in hell he can stay pissed off. He smiles and raises his glass.

"Thank you, my shaman, my rabbi. I'm glad you've been having fun. Maybe I should get a rebate."

After a good dinner and many bottles of much better champagne, our party is in good spirits. Maurice, a little drunk, stands:

"I have an announcement." Then he turns to Candy. "You

should do it, sweetheart." Candy—also feeling no pain at this point—stands and raises her glass.

"Maurice and I would like to announce the formation of On a Shoestring Pictures, an independent film company dedicated to high-quality, low-budget feature-length films. Documentaries and original feature films. I will be—excuse me—I am the president of the company and Maurice, my partner in life and in art, is the CEO and chief financial officer."

There are whoops and cheers around the table, more clinking of glasses, more drinking. In the melee, Herbie and Maurice catch each other's eye and nod. Good job, Maurice, is what Herbie's nod says, and Maurice acknowledges. Then Maurice takes Herbie's arm and pulls him close.

"She's changed, Herbie," he says softly in his ear. "She's ready to step into herself. Sometimes out of sadness . . ." He leaves the rest unsaid.

"How long are you guys staying? I'd like to have y'all over for dinner," says Roxanne.

"Just tomorrow," answers Candy. "We fly back to New York tomorrow night. Then first thing Wednesday morning I'm meeting with a decorator to design my office."

"First things first," says Maurice.

"Daddy, could you and I have lunch tomorrow? Before we leave?"

"I don't know—have your people call my people." He squeezes her arm.

"And I'd like to take Herbie's lesson with Billy, if that's all right. I brought my clubs."

"Excellent," says Billy. "How's 11:30?" Maurice nods. "Right at the same place we had the bad champagne," she adds.

"What about you, Roxanne? We left you out," says Candy.

"No, honey. I'm on zit patrol. I've got patients all day."

CHAPTER SIXTEEN

HERBIE IS NOT A BIG FAN OF CHAMPAGNE. IT'S OKAY while he's drinking it, but the next morning it always gives him a nasty second act. He needs coffee to get the blood moving again, so he gets dressed and heads out. There's a Dunkin' Donuts a little farther down the block than the Starbucks, but it's worth the extra steps. Starbucks pisses him off. If you want a small coffee you have to order the Tall. What the fuck is that all about?

He carries the coffee and a couple of plain old-fashioned donuts back to his room and hears the cell phone ringing while he's fiddling with the key. Well, not a key but one of those little plastic cards that he always puts in the wrong way. By the time he gets in, the phone has stopped. He looks at the little screen and he's surprised to see it was Jeffrey.

"My agent," he says when he calls him back. "My agent called me! It must be Christmas!"

"I hate to interrupt your vacation but I took a chance."

"What's up?"

"There's an independent film. I read it and it's not bad; very good part for you. It's twelve days' work, in New York; no money, of course, but I can get good billing. They want to meet with you—the writer/director and the producer—day after tomorrow."

"A meeting?"

Jeffrey sighs. "Yes."

"For what?"

"Maybe they want to see if you're still alive."

"That's why I have an agent—to tell people I'm still alive."

Jeffrey lets that pass.

"When?"

"Thursday."

"No, I'm all the way down here; I'm playing golf; there's no money . . ."

"I'm sorry, Herbie, I don't handle golfers. You want to be an actor, get on a plane and do the meeting."

"I don't think so."

Another silence.

"I don't know if I want to do this shit anymore, Jeffrey. Olive said something to me the other day that really hit me. She said she was past pretending. And I'm thinking, me, too. You know what I'm talking about?"

"You're in touch with Olive?"

"Yeah."

"How's she doing up there?"

"My guess? She's going to rip the roof off the place."

"Should I go?"

"Absolutely. And bring some people. Casting people. Once they see her in this, you can just sit there with your feet up on your desk and field the offers."

"I'll go first and see for myself—before I buy plane tickets for people. I'll go for the opening. You?"

"Yeah, the opening," says Herbie. "So, it's a good script, this movie? What's it about?"

"It's about a kid, what else? He has sex, he grows up; he has sex, he learns the ropes; he has sex."

"What am I, the father?"

"The boyfriend of the mother—a real character. It's a good role."

"The script is good?"

"I think it is. I'll fax it to you, if that fleabag you're staying in has a fax machine."

"No, if you think it's good, that's enough for me. Tell them to make an offer. No meeting."

Jeffrey pauses a moment. "All right. Why not? I'll tell them."

"FedEx the script and tell them I'll do it, but no meeting."

"Got it." He hangs up.

Maybe Herbie's past pretending; maybe he's not. But he still likes it when somebody wants to cast him in a movie. He notices that he feels a bit more pep in his step as he takes his shower and gets dressed to meet Candy for lunch. Somebody wants him and he's been an actor too long for that not to feel good.

They're lunching at the golf resort he hates because he knows it's the only place in town that Candy can make the kind of entrance she likes to make. Sure enough, he gets there twenty minutes before her, orders a Bloody Mary and waits. Then, when he sees all the heads in the restaurant turn, he knows his daughter has arrived. Elvis is in the building. He doesn't have to look.

"I love this place," she says as she kisses him on the top of the head and sits across from him. "It's like a fifties movie with Lana Turner, very country club." She looks great. There aren't many women who can make an outfit look as good as it does on Candy. And she did some shopping in Venice.

"Ooh, I'll have what you're having. What a good idea."

Herbie signals the waiter to bring two more Bloody Marys.

"You look happy," he says to her after she settles.

Candy puckers her mouth up to let Herbie know she's mulling something over. Bad acting, he thinks as he watches her.

"I feel almost guilty about it. Well, not almost. I feel guilty. But I am happy, Daddy."

"Why guilty?" he asks, but he knows why.

"I miss Mommy terribly. Every time I remember that she's gone, I feel devastated. But something good also happened to me."

"Yeah, Maurice mentioned something about it to me last night—about 'out of sadness . . .'"

"I'm sure there's all kinds of psychological explanations for what I'm feeling."

Herbie nods. Oh yes, he thinks. "It's normal," he says. "Suddenly there's space where there wasn't any before. Your mom took up a huge space."

"But I shouldn't be happy."

"Here's the thing: you're sad and you're happy. Both. You love your mother—we all know that. Give yourself a break. This morning, Jeffrey called with a movie and I hated the idea of acting again and I loved that somebody wanted me to act. Both—at the same time. That's the way we are. Let yourself off the hook."

"Thanks."

"I'm happy you're happy."

The waiter comes with menus and that gives them a chance to look away from each other. Neither of them has ever been comfortable with the father/daughter thing. Maybe because Herbie's way of dealing with women is to be direct—which works with pretty much every woman in the world except his daughter. She always looks at him like he's going to hit her. Ah, well.

"Have you spoken to Olive at all?"

Herbie nods, staying in the menu.

"I talked to her from Venice a couple of times. She's excited about the play."

"Yeah, I've spoken to her."

"We're flying up for the opening. You want to hitch a ride?"

"Sure," says Herbie, and his eyes flick away. Candy sees his evasion and pounces on it; she can read her father like a neon sign. "You're not waiting for the opening, are you? You're going to sneak up early and catch the first preview."

He shrugs.

"That's when you always went to see Mom. The first audience."

"Yeah, I prefer that."

"Why?"

"It's the first and the last pure show. It can get better after that but never purer. Once they hear the audience reaction, the actors remember how smart they are."

Herbie signals the waiter and they order lunch and a couple more drinks. After the waiter leaves, Candy leans in with elbows on the table.

"You're in love with Olive, aren't you, Pops? You've got a thing for Olive."

"Easy." He shrugs it away. He doesn't want to get into this with her. "I've been coaching her, that's all. I want to see how she does."

"Oh, Pop."

"Don't . . . don't do this. Don't make a drama where there isn't one."

"Oh, Pop."

"Stop saying that, all right?"

"She's too young for you."

"Of all the people in the world who might have that opinion, you are not eligible, I'm sorry."

Candy purses up her lips again—this time it means that Herbie is not being a gentleman to bring up the age difference between her and her betrothed.

"And I'm not in love with her. You're taking a big leap here."

"She's sleeping with Sam Harding."

"No, she's not."

"Daddy, she is. I talk to her all the time. She's bonking the director."

"She's not . . . bonking anybody."

And Candy gives him that look that says that women know things like this because when women talk to each other they tell the truth—not like when women talk to men. Herbie hates this look.

"Whatever," he says, and waves it away with his hand. But in fact, he's taken the bait and Candy has set the hook.

Maurice and Billy are waiting for them at the bar at the Fleetwood in North Myrtle. They have clearly had a bonding experience on the golf course and they're celebrating.

"Were you able to teach him anything?"

"No," says Billy. "But I learned a lot. Very interesting son-in-law you have there."

"I've invited Billy to the wedding," says Maurice to Candy. "If that's all right with you, of course. I'm thinking maybe she should perform the ceremony."

"That's a totally great idea," says Candy, "although I thought you said you didn't want a religious service."

"I'll tone it down," says Billy. "What I really want is a ride in the jet, but if I have to work for it, that's okay. Don't worry, I'll dress up nice."

"I'm not worried." And Candy gives Billy a big hug.

"You all right?" Maurice asks Herbie, who has been quiet.

"Yeah. What are you drinking?" They amble away from the women to the bar.

"You look like you've been hit by a truck."

"Lunch with the daughter."

"Oy. You guys all right?"

"We're crazy about each other but somehow we always manage to dish up a little pain. I don't know what it is. We'll be fine. Don't postpone the wedding." He glances over at Candy, who although deep into a conversation with Billy is fully aware of Herbie and Maurice and knows exactly what they're talking about at the bar. She sees Herbie looking at her and she sticks her tongue out at him. This is a sign that she wants to be friends again. Herbie blows her a kiss. What the fuck, he thinks, is she so angry about?

"Why don't you fly back with us?" asks Maurice. "You've made your point; you're a golfer. Come on home."

"Soon, soon."

"What do you want? Vodka?"

"Yeah."

Not long after that, the black cloud of Herbie rains out the party and everybody begs off—Maurice and Candy for the airport and Billy to clean her house. And Herbie moves into his bar stool on a more permanent basis. He's not sure he really believes that Olive is fucking Sam. Probably not, he thinks. Candy always goes for that first off—everybody's fucking everybody—judging the world by her own standards. But he starts to fantasize about it while he's sitting at the bar—what the hell, he thinks, I may as well get some juice out of this, too. It's a quarter to three; there's no one in the place, except you and me. He signals the barman for another double vodka rocks and he brings up a picture of Olive and Sam in bed. He has to create Sam out of his imagination because he has no idea what he looks like. But there they are, going at it good, Sam helping her to a long, deep come like only a young, strapping fellow can, Olive with her knees up around her ears. And even with the alcohol and the tiredness, Herbie feels that old feeling, that stirring in his shorts. That gets a smile. Years ago when Annie told him about her love affairs, he asked her to go into detail, which she did with her legendary aplomb. They both got so hot from the images she was pulling up that they fucked their brains out right there on the couch. You never know what gets you going.

He looks in his jacket pocket for his cell phone and, of course, it's not there. He goes out to the parking lot and finds his car and there's the phone, lying on the passenger seat. He gets in the car because it's chilly outside. He fills his pipe and takes a toke and punches in Roxanne's number.

"You busy?" he asks her.

"No, come on over. Can you drive?"

"Yeah, I'm fine."

A half hour later, Roxanne is down between his legs, giving him head and he's deep in thought. He's not happy about the way the evening is progressing. A blow job, for him, is not a good way to start things and he mentioned that to her. But she was hell-bent. Come here, darling, he said to her. Come up here; we'll take our time. But she went right for his cock. A blow job is not his favorite thing in general. I mean, under certain circumstances, when the mood is right, it can be wonderful. But to start out this way—cold—with no real pleasure coming from her yet, it's not his first choice. Not to mention he's had way too much to drink for the art of making love. He gets a kind of boozer's impotence, which means he has a raging hard-on but he won't be able to come for hours. So she's working her ass off down there, going for the Academy Award and all he can think about is how he's never going to come and she's going to think it's her fault and that she didn't do it right. God, he hates this.

"Sweetheart, come here, let me touch your pussy a little," he urges.

"No darlin', you have to let me do this. This is what I do best, so you have to let me shine."

What's he going to do? Say no? But it's not his favorite thing. Maybe it's the passive position; he's not easy with that. Just to lie there and be acted upon doesn't finally work for him. On the other hand, he likes to get straddled. He doesn't mind that—when the girl's in the driver's seat, going for it in her own way, at her own tempo. He likes that. But that's not really being passive. You're working hard down there—just facing uphill instead of down. But this position, lying back with your legs open, maybe resting on an elbow or reclining on pillows, watching her do you, it's like being diapered. That could be my problem, he thinks. Yeah, I think we're onto something.

Roxanne is starting to get the idea that he's not in paradise and starts to work harder. This is exactly what he's been dreading. She's going to make it her fault. She's going to fail and he's going to be the reason for her failure. He's going to be her judge, which he really, really, really doesn't want to be. I'm the guilty one, he's thinking; it's my fault, but he knows there's no way she's going to see it that way.

If only she didn't think she had to perform. What is this shit? Why can't we just fuck like monkeys? No posing, no pretense, just be exactly where you are, rubbing each other up, getting high on each other, laughing even. Oh God! Just letting go and being naked together and in love. Oh God.

It takes years to trust. Annie knew him like you know that old magazine you have in the basket by the toilet. You've already read it cover to cover but it's still the best one in the room. The two of them were free to play because they knew each other so well. Some days she'd have an itch, some days not—but she was great at starting from scratch. Or sometimes she'd be pissed at him for getting drunk the night before in front of well-dressed people—she hated when he did that. Or he had gotten stoned to go the PTA meeting, or some such shit. So she'd be pissed and there had to be a thawing-out period before she would let her pussy come out to play. And Herbie knew exactly how drunk he had been the night before and exactly how pissed she was, so he just let her talk it out, and he'd nod away with a hopeful look on his face until she let his thigh go up between her legs. And then she'd start to put a little pressure against it—only as much as she wanted to—no more. And he would start to make that sound in his throat that he likes to make when he starts to feel like Simba, the lion king. And then, and then.

You can't just start out with a person and have trust like that. Annie knew just what to say to make him come, for instance. She used one word when she wanted to make him come in seven strokes, and another when she wanted to make him come in eight. She could make him come in one, but that also included a gesture. She never figured out the right phrase for fifty-seven strokes. But when she was ready to be done, she whispered this or that, and then they were done. And there was no problem with that, no second-guessing. Done is done. I feel good. See you in the morning. That takes years.

Roxanne is now pulling out all her best stuff, so he tries to picture Olive and Sam doing it and that gets some feeling going. Olive is so spectacular, he thinks. He inserts himself, so to speak, in Sam's place and imagines the lovely smell coming up from her body as she heats up. Like bread in the oven. Yeah, he thinks, that's working. And Roxanne gets the message and adds her encouragement from down below. Come on, everybody, let's pull it together and get old Herbie over the fence! Come on, we can do it!

Afterward, he lies about how wonderful it was and she goes on about what a stud he is and how well endowed he is—which every man likes to hear whether it's bullshit or not.

"You're a sexy little devil, aren't you?" she says and he grunts like the caveman he is. "But you don't have a dime's worth of interest in me."

His eyes pop open. He's not going to have his golden moment of repose and that saddens him. It's the whole reason he does it, he thinks. "What are you talking about?"

"Okay, I know you like me a lot and I like you, but your mind is on another woman."

He starts to protest but she puts her hand over his mouth. "And don't tell me you're thinking about your dead wife. You've got another woman on your mind—a live one. Herbie, I am the world's foremost authority on being in bed with a man who's thinking about another woman. I know what I'm talking about."

Herbie decides not to protest anymore. He just lies there.

"Come on, tell me all about her."

And his phone rings. It's in the pocket of his pants and he didn't turn it off. It's got to be Olive. No one else would call him at this hour.

"That's her, isn't it? Well, go on, answer it! Tell her what a great blow job you just got."

CHAPTER SEVENTEEN

~

N O, HERBIE DOESN'T ANSWER THE PHONE. HE AND Roxanne lie there frozen, like two mice when the kitchen lights go on, listening to the ringing of his pants on the chair. When it stops they wait for it to ring again, which it does. Then the phone is quiet.

"And now she's leaving the message," says Roxanne. "And it's not going to be a nice one. You can just tell, can't you?"

Herbie has hit bottom.

"Havin' a bad night, hon?"

He has no words.

"Your girlfriend just caught you having sex that you didn't even like. That's what we call a bad night."

"I did like it," he mumbles.

"Oh come on. You want to be the one in charge; you want your hand on the throttle or you can't come. I'll tell you what, sweetheart, you ought to figure out how to let out your feminine side. Learn how to receive a little."

He just looks at her.

"Didn't your wife ever go down on you?"

He shouldn't get into this, he thinks, but . . . "Yeah, but she liked to do it when she was already coming herself, you know? She did it to jack up her pleasure. That's a whole different experience."

Roxanne's face looks like she's been clubbed with a lead pipe. Then Herbie watches her consider this information, reject it and then file it in a place where she'll never have to look at it again.

"I can't have a serious talk with you lying there with your dick out. I'm sorry. Go get dressed and meet me in the kitchen."

He puts on his underwear and socks.

"And I want to hear that message."

"No . . ."

She puts her finger in his face. "You listen to me: you used my body as your receptacle while you were thinking about your other girlfriend. So according to the Marquis of Queensbury Rules, you owe me big. I'm going to hear that message before you leave this house. That's the only fun I'm going to get out of this whole miserable night."

Dressed and downstairs, he fills the kettle and puts it on for tea. Roxanne comes down in a robe, looks at the kettle and goes to the bar and makes a drink. She fills a tumbler with ice and laces it with bourbon.

"All right, tell me all about her."

And Herbie does—all about the night in the bar when they met and how he took her to meet Annie in the hospital; and about how Annie and Olive spent the night talking while he walked the streets wishing he was a fly on the wall. He tells her about seeing Olive at the memorial service, when she seemed to be illuminated from the inside.

"How old?"

"Thirty-four."

"Oh, baby," she clucks. "Well, she'll outlive you—at least you won't have to worry about that. Play me the tape."

Herbie finds the message and puts the phone on speaker.

"Hi," says Olive's voice. Then there's a long silence. "I know what you're doing, Herbie. It's weird, but I can feel it. You're with Roxanne and you're . . . in bed with her. I can actually feel it in my body. Thanks a lot."

They listen to her think a moment.

"I don't know why you're doing this. I don't get why you feel you have to push yourself away from me. I'm not a scary person."

She's crying. "This hurts. I didn't know you could hurt me so much. I didn't see that coming.

"I don't have the time to deal with this right now. I have to open a show and you have officially become a distraction. So don't call me anymore, okay?" She lets this sink in. "I'll talk to you soon," and she disconnects. Herbie and Roxanne share a smile.

"Play it again," says Roxanne, and he does.

"She sounds like a nice person. I was all ready to scratch her eyes out but she's nice; you can tell. And pretty grounded for a thirty-four-year-old."

"She is."

"Real good-looking, I'll bet."

He nods.

"You knew she was going to call, didn't you?

He did. Of course he did. They've been speaking every night. Of course he knew she was going to call.

"So what's that all about?"

Olive would have stuck to her guns about not calling Herbie were it not for the crisis surrounding Bob's breakdown. His fall into psychosis happens over the period of a week and it's frightening for Sam and the actors to watch. At first they think that his eccentric behavior is intentional, an actor's ploy to get deeper into the role. But by the third day he slips further into the murk of Vanya's psyche and he loses control. Sam has a meeting with the producers and shares his concern and they decide to inquire into finding a backup for Bob if, indeed, things get worse. They call an actor who has recently played Vanya in a production in Minneapolis. He says that he's free and they send him the new translation so that he can get familiar with it.

Bob is in a state of self-imposed isolation; he murmurs to himself when he stands offstage waiting to enter for a scene or sings Russian lullabies softly in the men's dressing room, where he has built a tent in the corner out of bedsheets he brought from his apartment. After the first dress rehearsal he starts wearing parts of his costume home and word is getting around that he's not been washing. He is inaudible at this afternoon's run-through and he disappears before the notes session and no one can find him for hours. Finally Olive goes to the bench in the park where they used to eat lunch and finds him there, crying softly in the rain. She leads him back to theater like an invalid and helps to change him into dry clothes. Then she calls Herbie.

"I'm glad you called," he says.

"We have a big problem here and I thought maybe you could help," she replies with no warmth in her voice.

"Sure."

"It's Bob. He's losing it and Sam thinks he may have to replace him with an actor from Minneapolis, and . . ."

"Sam's wrong," snaps Herbie. "Tell your brilliant young director he would be making a stupid mistake if he tries to get another actor."

"Why do you have that tone in your voice? Don't you dare snap at me. I'm the one who's supposed to be angry."

"Leave him alone. Leave Bob alone and he'll be fine."

"You don't understand. He's disintegrating. He's not going to make it."

"Shall I describe it to you?" says Herbie. "He's built a tent in the dressing room so no one can see him, right?"

Olive is silent.

"He stares off into space and doesn't listen to anybody. He's wearing his character's underwear and it's starting to smell. How am I doing so far?"

"Pretty accurate."

"Just leave him alone; he'll be fine—better than fine. My guess is he's going to be brilliant. Has he started that shrieky laughter yet? That's the worst. You have to leave the room when he does that."

"He's refusing to take any notes from Sam. He calls them speed bumps."

"That's not crazy."

"What do you mean?"

"Do you like getting notes now?"

"Sam's trying to make the play better. It's mostly just little tweaks, but they can be important, no?"

"No. It's all bullshit. Right now you're in a wrestling match. The actors are ready to take the play and the director can't bear to give it up yet. So these notes, these tweaks, are just a way for Sam to justify his rapidly diminishing existence as the director of the play. Tell him to leave Bob alone."

"So Bob does this every time he's in a show?"

"Some version of it. Maybe playing Vanya has made it more intense."

"And people hire him?"

"Not much anymore, which is a shame. He's brilliant."

"And totally crazy."

"If you think this is crazy you should see how he behaves in life. He's a fucking lunatic."

"He's your best friend."

181

He grunts and there's a silence.

"There's another aspect to this that I should warn you about," he says. "There's a darker side to these breakdowns."

"Darker than this?"

"Annie did a play with him years ago and he did his breakdown number like this just before the play opened. Everyone hovered and worried and stumbled through rehearsals trying to hear him; and then the play opened and Bob was brilliant and the rest of the actors had lost a step. And they were all pretty pissed off, as I recall, when the reviews came out."

"Oh my God."

"Yeah. Warn the other people."

There's a pause.

"Why did you do it, Herbie?"

He sighs.

"No, why?"

"It's not going to sound like much of an explanation."

"Try me."

"Candy and Maurice came down here to South Carolina; she and I had lunch and she told me that you were bonking Sam—her word. And it . . . made me a little crazy."

"Candy?"

"After they left, I got drunk and sat there at the bar, picturing the two of you in the act. You were naked and very hot and I got . . . you know, aroused—right there at the bar. So I picked up the phone and called Roxanne. It was a deeply stupid and self-destructive thing to do, but that was my frame of mind at the moment, and . . ."

"You sprung a woodie thinking about me naked?"

"I did."

Another pause.

"I think that's your first real declaration of love."

He smiles. "It's not exactly Be My Valentine."

"I'm not bonking anybody."

"Not even Sam?"

"Not even you."

He thinks about that.

"Candy is weird," she says.

"Oh yeah."

"I mean, Jesus! She likes to giggle on the phone about boys—you know, like teenagers do, so I told her about how cute Sam is with his cute little ass in those tight jeans—that kind of crap. And out of that she tells you I'm having sex with him?"

"Uh-huh."

"And you believed it."

"I think I wanted to. I wanted to wallow in it, get drunk and listen to sad songs. I can be an asshole like that sometimes. And then to make myself feel worse, I went and humiliated myself with Roxanne."

"Were you too drunk?"

"It was sad in a lot of ways."

"Did it depress you?"

"Yes."

"Good."

He smiles.

"I got a job," he tells her.

"A play?"

"A movie. It's not official yet but I'll get the offer today."

"How do you know?"

"Jeffrey would never have agreed to demand an offer if he didn't know I would get it. He would never put me in that position. Jeffrey, you'll see, is very protective of his people and their egos."

"That's nice. Is he going to come up?"

"For the opening."

"If we have an opening."

"Bob Frankel has been wanting to play this part for thirty-five years. He's not going to miss it. Just warn everybody to watch out for themselves."

"I'll tell Sam."

"Oh, Sam again."

"Bye."

Herbie finds the number of Olive's theater and buys a single ticket for the first preview on Friday night. He gets on the motel's computer and prints out directions from South Carolina to Rochester, New York—fourteen hours or so of driving. If he leaves early this afternoon he'll even have time to stop for some sleep. He calls Billy to tell her he's leaving and they make a plan to have a cup of coffee before he gets on the road.

He starts throwing his things into the suitcase and the phone rings.

"Herb Aaron, please."

"Speaking."

"Mr. Aaron, my name is Sam Harding. I'm the director of *Uncle Vanya* in Rochester?"

"Yes, Sam, I know who you are. You're calling about Bob?"

"Yes. I'm terrified that he won't be able to perform the play. We have our first audience tomorrow night."

"No, he'll be okay."

"Olive just told me you said that, but are you sure?"

"I am."

"Are you absolutely certain?" He stresses every syllable.

Herbie smiles. "You're not convinced."

"No, frankly. I think he's truly lost it."

"How about when he's onstage?"

"Who knows? We can't hear a bloody word he's saying. Even the actor standing right next to him can't hear him."

"Get an audience in there and you'll hear him just fine. He's a crafty old coot. Watch your back and make sure you protect the other actors."

"How?"

"Don't let them get sucked down into his hole. Rehearse all the scenes he's not in. Get them juiced up about opening their play. You know what to do."

"Are you coming?"

"Are you kidding? *Uncle Vanya* without the uncle? I wouldn't be caught dead within a thousand miles of that theater."

"That's not even faintly amusing."

"No, I'll be there. Opening."

"How can I believe you know what you're talking about? What if you're wrong? My God, I feel as if I'm hanging over a vast, dark pit; I'm about to plunge in and I have no idea what's waiting for me at the bottom."

"Really," says Herbie.

CHAPTER EIGHTEEN

THE QUESTION IS THE GOLF CLUBS. HIS PLAN HAD BEEN to take them to the drop-off at the St. Andrews golf resort and leave them—shoes, glove, balls, tees, the whole thing—and just drive off. A symbolic gesture. But now he's thinking maybe not. Ever since that night when Billy told him to quit he's actually been enjoying the game.

"What the fuck," he thinks and hoists them into the trunk of the car next to his suitcase. He locks the car and walks down to Dunkin Donuts to get a coffee, feeling an odd sense of freedom. He has no idea what he's free from but it's like he's lost twenty pounds. Maybe it's the drive, the anticipation of motion, the leaving of one place for another. Maybe it's the morning, which has more than a hint of spring in it. Whatever the reason, he feels good. Almost as good, he thinks, as if he had lost the twenty pounds.

He carries his coffee back to the motel and stops in the office to go over his bill and the clerk hands him a package—the movie script from Jeffrey. He feels the weight of it in his hand, gently bouncing it up and down. What's it about? He thinks of the old joke. It's about a pound and a half. Chick-a-boom. He goes to his room and flicks through it, finding his scenes, which are not bad. He could have fun with this. He calls Jeffrey.

"What's the story? Do we have an offer?"

"We do."

"So when were you going to tell me?"

"I'm still working on the billing. There's no more money to squeeze out of them so we may as well go to war over the billing."

Herbie doesn't care all that much about billing. If he's good in the movie he'll get noticed; if he's not he won't. It doesn't really matter where his name is or how big it is on the credit roll.

"I can get you third place—after the kid and the girlfriend—or I can get you an 'And Herb Aaron' at the end, which I think is much better. It stands out more."

"Who's the kid again?"

"He's on a TV show."

He grunts. "And the girl?"

"Her, too."

"And they really think these kids can put asses in seats?"

"Oh definitely."

"And I can't."

"Well, maybe an old ass or two."

"See if you can get me a but."

"I beg your pardon."

"At the end of the credits, it should say, 'But Herb Aaron.'"

"Call me when you're sober." And Jeffrey hangs up.

When he's all packed and ready to go, he drives over to the Fleetwood to meet Billy. She's at her bar stool—third from the left—with a double espresso in front of her. Herbie signals for the same and gives her a kiss on the forehead before he sits down.

"Oh, I'm gonna miss you," she says.

"Me, too, you."

"We don't get people like you down here very often."

"Disgruntled assholes?"

"You know what I mean."

They take a moment to silently acknowledge how crazy they are about each other.

"I'm sorry that I had to get Roxanne mixed up in my mess. I didn't do very well by her."

"She's fine. She's been talking about it all week. She has herself cast as the femme fatale in the whole drama."

"She was; she is."

"And you jolted her loose a little bit, which she needed."

"From what?"

"From that steel rod she had up her ass about men. She was well on her way to being a lonely woman but I think you helped her change direction. She's feeling sexy again."

"She is sexy. Tell the next guy that comes along to watch out. He's gonna have a lot of woman on his hands."

"Yep," says Billy, who seems forlorn.

"What's up?"

"Oh, I'm okay."

"No, you're not."

She smiles. "I don't know. I think your leaving's got me feeling like I'm sitting still."

"Are you?"

"Worse—I'm sitting in a hole. When Mari died I poured myself into my work, which turned out to be a great way to find out what a stupid piece of shit my work is."

"Teaching?"

"Golf. I mean, Jesus. Hitting a little ball into a little hole? What's that? Maybe when it wasn't my whole life it was okay— kind of a lark, teaching people something they'll never be able to do and we all get a good laugh out of it—that's fine. But when it's the only thing on God's earth that I'm about, that I'm defined by—it's a bad joke."

"You're starting to sound like me."

"Well, it's all your fault. You got me going."

"What are you going to do about it?"

"I don't know." Then after a short pause, "I did have a thought."

He just listens.

"Maybe I'll ask Candy and Maurice for a job in their film company."

"Oh yeah?"

"You know, at some starter level, like an apprentice of some kind. I've got some money saved up; they wouldn't have to pay me much. I could learn a whole new business, live in a whole new place with different people; just shake things up a bit, you know?"

Herbie purses his lips and looks into his coffee cup.

"You don't like it," says Billy.

"No, I do. You could do it for sure—brilliantly I imagine. It'd be a hoot to have you in New York. No, it's a great idea."

"I'm hearing a but."

He thinks about how to say it. "It's not about the place, Billy." She looks at him like she knows exactly what's coming. "You're a lover," he says. "And you don't have anybody to love."

After that there's not much to say. They have a big hug and promise to see each other soon, at the wedding. Then Herbie gets in the car and rolls out of Myrtle Beach. His plan is to make a lot of miles by this evening and then he'll have an easy drive up to Rochester tomorrow. Today, he'll clear the Baltimore Beltway, find a motel north of the city somewhere and crash. Just as he gets on the interstate and up to speed, the phone rings.

"Where are you?" It's Maurice.

"Driving out of town. Why?"

"Candy wants to talk to you."

"Put her on."

"No. She says she has to talk to you in person."

"Why in person?"

"She'll explain it to you."

"Oh Jesus Christ, Maurice, just tell her to call me."

He gets no reply.

"Look, I don't want to cast any aspersions on your wife-to-be, but she has never been able to do anything in a simple way. I'm in the car all day; just tell her to call me."

"Let her do it her way, will you? This is how she wants to do it."

"You guys are coming to Rochester for the opening, aren't you? I'll talk to her then. In person."

"No, it won't hold that long."

"What is it? What's so important? You tell me."

"It's something that came up for her this week with her shrink and then she and I kicked it around a bit. She's hit on something about herself and she wants to talk to you about it."

Herbie doesn't like the sound of this at all. Candy can get totally indulgent with her psychological stuff and it's always about something that he did wrong when she was a child. He'll have to sit there and apologize and tell her he understands how difficult that must have been for her to be his daughter. He hates that shit.

"She felt bad when we left you the other day," adds Maurice. "I know you were upset after your lunch together and Candy was, too. She said she felt like she had hurt you and she didn't understand why she did it. That's what started this whole thing, so she wants to square it with you."

"What are you, her attorney?"

"Yeah, I'm on the clock."

"What do you want me to do?"

"Ditch the car and I'll send the plane for you. We can have dinner together in New York; then they'll fly you up to Rochester tomorrow. It'll be easier on you, too."

"No, no. I'm not flying in the plane. I need my car up there anyway. No, I'm driving to Rochester."

"You need to do this for her, Herbie."

"Is this what kind of son-in-law you're going to be? Hocking me all the time?"

"Where are you stopping tonight?"

"North of Baltimore somewhere."

"I'll get back to you."

Ten minutes later the phone rings again.

"Okay," says Maurice. "There's a town called Cockeysville. I swear to God, that's the name."

"I know Cockeysville."

"Oh, the world traveler. You should get there between eight and nine tonight. There's a Ramada Inn right at the Cockeysville exit—there's only one. You have a room booked. We'll meet you at a bar called the Hitching Post, right up the road. They have burgers and shit like that."

"How'd you get all this? Your guy the spy?"

"I can't divulge. Be there by nine."

"This is a lot of shit to go through, Maurice. For what?"

"Look, if you don't know that you want to straighten things out with your daughter as much as she does with you, then you don't know yourself very well."

"Straighten out what?" He's getting exasperated.

"You know when she looks at you with that look that drives you nuts? I've seen her give you the look and I've seen your response to it. You know what I'm talking about."

Herbie chews on that. "Yeah, maybe. And this going to be about that?"

"That's what I think, yeah."

"What are you going to do, drive all the way from New York?"

"Helicopter. We'll fly back right after you and Candy have your talk and you can get drunk and stoned and go to sleep."

A helicopter, he thinks. Perfect. Now she's the star of her own Fellini movie.

Nine hours later, Herbie's in the bar. He's already put down a burger and three vodkas and he's feeling pretty good. The drive was easy and he made good time. He's already checked in, showered and shaved, and now he's sitting alone at a table for four in the back. The Hitching Post is a typical bullshit-cowboy place. Herbie's been in a million of them. There's sawdust on the floor, a jukebox with country songs, the beer is in pitchers, and the waitresses are all dressed up like little cowgirls. All total bullshit. Why can't a bar just be a bar, he wonders. In Italy or France, a bar is a bar, a restaurant is a restaurant. They don't have a theme; they don't have costumes; they don't have a list of cute drinks that relate to the theme in some way. Like the Buckaroo. I'd have to be pretty fucking loaded to drink something called the Buckaroo. They better come soon, he thinks, or I'm going to go to bed.

Then, at the exact stroke of nine, he sees them come in and the guy at the bar points them over. They've both tried to dress way down but it's obvious their clothes are worth more than the whole building. Candy is nervous. Herbie can see it from across the room. She's not crazy about this place and she's letting Maurice know it.

"Jesus," she says when she gets to the table, "maybe we should have done this over the phone."

Herbie raises his eyes to Maurice, who shrugs. "I'm going to leave you guys to yourselves. I'll be at the bar. Be nice to each other." And he takes himself around to the far side of the bar.

"He's been great about this," says Candy as she sits across from Herbie.

"Yeah, a helicopter."

"Proves he really loves me, huh?"

"Or that he's trying to kill you."

She kicks him under the table. "Don't even say that."

"You want a drink?"

"No. And you could slow down a little, too. I'd like you to actually hear this."

Oh shit, he thinks. This is going to be awful.

"Anyway, Maurice is responsible for this. He pushed it. He doesn't like it that we don't like each other."

"Tell him we do."

"I was pretty nasty to you about Olive the other day, telling you that she's seeing the director."

"Seeing?"

"Well, you know. I don't know why I did that and when I told Maurice, he said—in his typical way—'What is this shit between the two of you? Can't you do something about it?' So I did. I went back to Dr. Pelzner."

"And she thinks I was a bad father, right?"

"She knows you were a bad father. She's known that for years. She's already published a whole paper about that. This is something else."

Herbie takes a big pull on his drink and braces himself. Then he gestures with his hands—come on, give it to me.

"Okay." She takes a breath. "You know the myth, the family myth?"

"What myth is that?"

"You know. That mom was the center of it all, the source of all the stuff that made our life so fantastic?"

He nods. This is making him nervous.

"That's the story I grew up with. You sold it to me like other parents sell the Catholic Church or the Bible. I cut my teeth on it. And I have to tell you, Daddy, it sucked."

"What do you mean?"

"Well, first of all, can you imagine how intimidating that was? How confusing it was to a little girl? How could I ever live up to that, you know?"

He nods, reluctantly.

"And second—and this the worst part—it wasn't fucking true! You made it up. You sold me a load of crap. This . . . myth . . . was something that you needed to be true for some reason. That Mom was the source; Mom was the genius; Mom was everything to everybody. I mean, don't get me wrong, she was great—amazing."

Her eyes fill with tears.

"But she wasn't the source of our good life, Daddy. You were. You were the one who made the Ferris wheel go around. And Mom thought so, too. She said without you, her life would have been pretty dull."

"When did she say that?"

"Not long ago. Just before she died. All those things we did, the amazing places we went, the brilliant people we hung out with all the time. It wasn't her, Daddy; it was you."

He shakes his head.

"I used to sit there when I was a kid and watch you do it. You always started with her—you lit her up about some idea, some trip, some new adventure; you got her going. You rubbed her up like Aladdin's lamp until she shined like gold. And then whatever you wished for just showed up for us—seemingly out of nowhere. It was magic."

"I didn't have any magic."

"You did, Pop. Especially with the girls. They couldn't resist you. Still can't. Every actress you ever worked with, the wives of all your friends—remember Sarah Ruskin? I mean my God, that woman was as boring as dirt until you walked into the room."

"Well she was an outrageous flirt."

"Only with you, Pop. And remember my friend Sylvia?"

"I never flirted with your friends."

"No, her mother—remember her? She had a big thing for you."

"She was actually a problem, as I recall."

"You have a gift, Daddy. Admit it. And you did too flirt with my friends! Are you kidding? Like all of them. I don't mean you came on to them or anything creepy like that. You just liked to light them up—like the bulbs on a Christmas tree. It's always been so easy for you. When I was little, you made them giggle; when I got bigger, you made them blush."

"Well . . ."

"You did, Daddy. All the girls except me."

Herbie sits frozen.

"That's the other part I want to talk with you about."

"What?"

"How you never did that for me. Every other girl except me."

"You're my daughter, for God's sake. I can't . . . that's child abuse."

"I don't know. Maybe. I've talked to the shrink about it and rationally it makes perfect sense that you wouldn't, but that doesn't mean it didn't hurt."

"Honey . . ."

"And make me feel like the only unattractive woman in the world."

"Sweetheart."

She starts to cry. "Or the only unattractive little girl in the world, which is worse. I kept trying to figure out how to get you to look at me like that. I was smart at school; I was funny when you had people to dinner. I did cartwheels. Nothing worked."

"Honey, let me say something."

"It was like I was invisible to you."

"No . . ."

"And the more I tried, the more you looked away."

"Honey, let me say something."

"What did I have to do, Daddy?"

"Can I talk? Please?"

She looks at him and purses her lips.

"I hate it when people say that," she says.

He laughs out loud. He loves this girl.

"What?" she says impatiently. "What do you want to say? You have the floor."

"You *were* lit up when you were a kid. You didn't need me to light anything. You did it all on your own. You always have."

"You're not hearing me. I'm talking about your attention. Your attention to me. You were so generous with all those other people—those other girls, I should say—and so . . . niggling . . . with me. So, what the fuck was *that* all about? To quote a famous father."

He shakes his head. He doesn't know.

"I'm not asking you to do anything, Daddy. You're not going to change; you're too old. This isn't for you; it's for me. It's good for me to say these things to you after all these years of thinking them and keeping them in. It makes me feel better. That's all I care about."

He has nothing to say.

"So go and find Olive. It's fine with me. It really is. I knew it was happening the first moment I saw her in Mom's room at the hospital. It was obvious. To Mom, too."

"What? You thought I was coming on to her? Because . . ."

"No. I thought she was coming on to you."

Maurice has been watching from the bar and when he senses they're done he comes over.

"So? It's good? You talked it out?"

They both nod.

"Good. I feel better."

Candy reaches across the table and takes Herbie's hand. "Thanks for listening, Pop."

"I love you, sweetheart."

"Who knew?" says Maurice. "That in the tiny hamlet of Cockeysville, words would be spoken that will echo down through all eternity."

CHAPTER NINETEEN

THERE'S GOOD NEWS AND BAD NEWS AT THE THEATER today—and it's all Bob. He shows up to rehearsal—the last before tonight's audience—and behaves as if nothing strange has happened at all, as if he's not been in a psychotic trance for the past five days. He's affable, even outgoing to everyone; he's the complete professional. He's washed himself, his clothes are clean, the tent in the dressing room has come down and his performance in rehearsal is as good as ever. Well, better actually. They're focusing primarily on Vanya's scenes because they were the least rehearsed during Bob's "illness" and Sam and the actors can't help but notice that his performance has deepened to a very profound level. Vanya's rages that had been impotent tantrums last week are now desperate pleas for attention and help. His self-loathing is now so intense that it's difficult for the others to watch. It's too painful, too naked. And yet, strangely enough, it's quite funny. And with that little paradox Bob is teaching a Master Class in the art of performing Chekhov.

Many of the other actors—Alvin McConnell among them—are outraged that Bob's crisis has been used to make his performance so much better than theirs. They feel they've been hoodwinked and they're not wrong. There's talk of bringing Bob up on charges before Equity, but going to the actors' union to complain that one member of the cast's performance is too good would be a tough sell.

Olive's response is something quite different. She's never before been in such close proximity to great acting and it thrills her right down to her high-button shoes. In her rehearsal with Bob she can't help but be a better actress. His rawness, his reckless courage, his commitment to the depth of Vanya's demons inspire her to meet his performance with everything she's got. She has no time to hesitate; she has no place to hide. It's the most alive she's ever felt in her life.

By the end of rehearsal, Sam is in heaven. His production is brilliant. He delivers his pep talk before they all break for dinner but there's not much left to say. "Think of tonight as another rehearsal," he says. "Just keep working the way you have been for the last four weeks. It's just another run-through."

And that's when the shrieking laughter starts—pretty much on schedule, as Herbie had predicted. The sound coming from Bob is not laughter. You couldn't call it that. Because there's no joy in it, no generosity, no fun; only an unearthly wail that makes you want to run from the room. It always starts with an interjection, shouted out by Bob, often in the form of a question—in this case, it's "Just another rehearsal?" And then the shrieking starts. No one knows what to do about it. No one wants to stay in the room, so finally Sam calls the dinner break and all the actors flee as if there were a fire.

"Hey, pretty," says Bob to Olive on her way out. "That was a fun scene, huh?"

Olive actually blushes, like she's been caught having sex behind the woodshed.

"Never knew it could be that good, huh?"

"I never did know that," she admits.

"What would your famous Herbie say if he saw that?"

"He would say it was pretty good, I think."

"And he'd be right, too," says Bob, suddenly the peacock.

"What are you doing for the break?" asks Olive.

"Napping in the dressing room."

"You can't eat?"

"Are you kidding?"

"But you can sleep?"

"No, but it's easier to pretend I'm sleeping than it is to pretend I'm eating. You?"

"I'll go home," says Olive, "and pretend to have some soup."

"Pretend soup!" he screams, followed by the despicable laughter. Olive waves and gets out of earshot as soon as she can.

Her apartment's not big enough to pace in. Two steps I'm bumping into the other wall, she thinks. It's too cold outside to take a walk. She flicks on CNN and flicks it off again. World? What world? Her well-worn script is on the kitchen counter but she doesn't want to look at it anymore. Words on a page, she thinks. She starts to silently go through her first scene, remembering her moves around the stage, but she stops herself. That's the worst thing I can do—play the scene in my mind without the other actors. That's terrible. "Herbie! Where are you?" she wails out loud. "Where are you when I need you?"

They had made a pact the day before—no contact twenty-four hours before the first preview. This way she would be purified, Herbie said, like a Jewish woman going to the mikvah before her wedding ceremony. Which is all well and good except that she really needs to talk to him. He would know how to get her to the stage tonight in one piece, without having an emotional breakdown, without breaking out in a rash. God, she thinks, why am I in this business?

* * *

Around this time, Herbie pulls up to his hotel. He's decided to go upscale for a change and try a hotel with room service instead of having to depend on those plastic coffeemakers in his room that turn out perfect cups of plastic coffee. This place is a chain, too—just a fancier chain. Now he's got a couple of hours to kill before the show. What to do? Ordinarily he'd take a walk but he doesn't want to chance running into Olive or Bob or somebody who would recognize him. He'd hit the bar but that's also problematic. If he drinks or smokes weed he'll sleep through the show, sure as hell. Doesn't make any sense, he thinks, to drive eight hundred miles just to cop a snooze in an uncomfortable seat. So what to do?

He turns on the tube and then switches it off again. Those fucking gas bags on the news shows. It's the biggest collection of bad acting in the history if the world, he thinks. This one's got his opinion and that one's got his and they're pretending to disagree with each other so that the show will have tension. "Give me a fucking break," he says out loud. "Get a job." So what to do?

He takes a shower, shaves, and sits on the couch in his robe—he's got a little suite-ette that's supposed to fool you into thinking you actually have two rooms. He sits there and thinks about last night with Candy. It was a shock to hear her say that about Annie—about how she wasn't the source of the juice. If Candy has to have it that way, fine. But it's more complicated. It's a deal between two people to live an extraordinary life.

But the other thing she said is eating at him. The thing about how he had to light up all those women, rub them up and make them shine. Especially Annie. What the fuck is that all about? Why is it his job to make women smile? I mean it doesn't take Sigmund Freud to know where that comes from—all those years of playing the cakewalking minstrel boy for his mother so that she wouldn't go insane and decimate their lives. Only little

Herbie could make her smile, make her forget the devil inside her. Are we old enough yet to get rid of that shit?

"Jesus," says Olive and she puts on her coat and goes to the theater. If she stays in her apartment another minute she's going to jump out the window. At least at the theater she can pace. Now it's six fifteen, almost two hours before the show starts. Jessica Alsop, the actress playing Sonia, is at the theater when Olive gets there. Jessica is a chronic sufferer and a dimwit and Olive hasn't had much use for her, but any port in a storm at this point.

"Hi," says Olive. "You nervous, too? I couldn't sit in my apartment any longer. It was driving me crazy."

"No, I never get nervous."

Oh fuck you, thinks Olive. I need help here for God's sake.

"I mean why should people in the audience make any difference to our work? We're not doing it for them. This is for us and for our art—and for our director. Sam would be disappointed if he knew you were nervous. You have nothing to prove to these people."

It's no secret that Jessica has a big crush on Sam and his attention to Olive has been a gnawing source of aggravation for her.

"So if you're not nervous, why are you here so early?"

"I just love it here, Olive. I love all theaters. I love to sit in the quiet and dark of the empty stage and listen to all the ghosts who have left their energy here. I want to suck up all their history and their knowledge and their wisdom."

Suck this, thinks Olive. And she would have made the appropriate gesture, too, if she didn't have to share a dressing room with this jerk for four more weeks. She puts her coat back on and goes for a walk. Even freezing to death is better than this.

* * *

Herbie's pacing now, too. What if she's no good? he thinks. What if she can't act? That would be that. It sounds stupid. I mean why would one thing have anything to do with the other, but it would. It would be a lie between them, slowly choking off any real feeling. There's nothing worse than a bad actress, he thinks. Like fingernails on a chalkboard. He'd rather shack up with a dental hygienist.

At seven thirty Herbie feels safe to leave the hotel. Half an hour before the show the actors have to be backstage and signed in—it's an Equity rule, so he won't run into anybody. It's only a few blocks from his hotel, so he takes his time, checking out the neighborhood for bars. He's trying to figure out where the actors go after the show. It'll be some place where the drinks are cheap and the burgers are good—if such a place exists in this town.

Turns out there are a lot of bars. This is a drinking town, he thinks, which makes sense. I mean what else are they going to do? There's one place that has wood-fired pizza, but it's too collegiate-looking for actors. There's a gay bar; there's a place that serves barbecue. And then he finds it. It's a couple of blocks too far from the theater to be perfect but he'll bet anything this is the hangout after the show. There's a 60s/70s feeling about the place, mixed in with a Moose Lodge kind of décor. The beer is cheap; the shots are cheap; and if you believe the menu outside they have the best burger in town. If this ain't the place, he thinks, it should be.

Backstage at the theater, it's eerily quiet. All the actors are staring at themselves in their mirrors, not quite sure they like what they see. There's a lot of sighing, little mmm's and aaahs to make sure there's no mucus on their vocal chords. The women are redoing their makeup, taking it all off and putting it on again. There's some stretching going on—especially in the ladies' dressing room. None of this means anything—their vocal chords are fine; their makeup is fine; their bodies are stretched. They're just terrified.

Then over the intercom comes the voice of the assistant stage manager: "Five minutes, ladies and gentlemen. Five minutes to curtain for Act One." There's a silence as each actor, in his or her own way, faces the void. And then Bob's voice pierces the silence—"Five minutes?" he screams, followed by the maniacal laughter. The other actors in his dressing room lunge for the door, all of them reaching it at the same time, like the Keystone Kops.

Herbie picks up his ticket and unobtrusively goes to his seat. He looks around to see if he can find Sam, but he's not at the director's traditional spot, standing at the back of the house. He must still be backstage, pestering the actors, thinks Herbie. There should be a law. Actually, he remembers, there is—an Equity rule that the director may not be backstage after half hour. But it's rarely enforced.

Then Herbie spots him coming out of a door to the side of stage left, followed by a pretty young woman carrying a clipboard. That's his trusty assistant, no doubt, ready to jot down any pearl that may fall from his lips. He's a good-looking, earnest fellow, thinks Herbie. Quite young. Too young, he thinks.

The houselights dim to half and the audience gathers itself. Then there's the obligatory announcement about cell phones, followed by beeping, ringing, and jingling sounds. Then all is silent for a moment and the houselights fade to black. In the darkness a mandolin begins to play; then it's joined by a concertina and a gypsy fiddle. It's a folk song—by Glinka, bets Herbie to himself. There's always a bump when you move from one reality to the other, and the director's job is to smooth out that bump as best he can, make it seem natural to leave one reality—your long, frustrating day at the office, for example, or the fight you just had with your wife—and let yourself slip into the stage world, where people pretend to be other people and say words that were written a hundred years ago by yet another person. This music helps a lot, thinks Herbie. It cushions the bump.

The stage lights come up and Herbie finds himself rigid with tension. He hates going to the theater. He'd rather have an electric cattle prod up his ass. The actors seem false, the words are stilted, the scenery is flimsy and fake. Who needs this shit? I could be in a bar somewhere. All right, he says to himself, lighten up, take a breath.

About ten minutes in, Olive makes her entrance as Yelena. She has no lines in this scene; she's just returning from a walk with some of the other characters, but Herbie senses something's off. She's fakey. She's working too hard. He has to fight an urge to stand up and tell her to start over again. Leave the stage, he wants to yell out; take a minute and enter again. It was always like this when he went to see Annie. He must have done it a hundred times and he never got used to it. Oh shit, he used to think when Annie came onstage, you're not going to try *that*. You're not going to play her like *that*, are you? It's so weird to watch someone you know intimately, someone you love, altering her rhythms, her speech patterns, her very psyche to fit into this other strange person. Weird. But Annie always brought him around. She was such a good actress she made him forget Annie altogether in a few minutes. Annie wasn't there on the stage at all—just this other broad.

Then he notices that his shoulders have dropped down from his ears and he's breathing normally. We're into a scene in the sitting room now. Yelena is working the room, not saying much— not needing to say much—flirting, being bored, occasionally reproaching Vanya for his boorish behavior. Her presence dominates the scene. She's good, he thinks. She's very good.

CHAPTER TWENTY

A FTER THE CURTAIN CALL, WHICH IS WILDLY ENTHUSIAS-tic, Herbie makes his way over to Sam, who is in deep conversation with some producer-looking types. Herbie waits to the side as the rest of the audience files out and finally Sam looks in his direction with a quizzical expression on his face. Where do I know this guy from? And then the penny drops.

"Of course, Herb Aaron. I never put the name with the face. I'm a fan of your work."

Herbie nods. He never knew how to take a compliment, so he turns it around.

"It's a brilliant evening, Sam. You've done a beautiful job."

"Oh my God, thank you. It really did pull together tonight amazingly well. This week has been . . . well, you know. Thanks for being so adamant about Bob. If it had been left to me I would have fired him—and we would have had, well . . . *Uncle Vanya* without the uncle, as you said. Anyway, thank you again."

"He's a piece of work, isn't he?"

"My God, I'd hate to see the inside of his head—all serpents and vipers, slithering around in the muck."

"But I don't think I've ever seen a better Vanya."

"No, he's extraordinary—absolutely extraordinary. And you must be delighted with your protégée. A star is born, no?"

"She's nobody's protégée," he says with a proud shake of his head. "But yeah, she's wonderful. She's a total actress, isn't she? The whole package."

"How *do* you know each other, by the way? Have you worked together? Are you related somehow?"

"We met in a bar."

Sam waits for more of an explanation but that's all he gets.

"Is that the way back?" asks Herbie, pointing to the door he saw Sam come out of earlier. Then, without waiting for a response, he heads backstage.

There are only two dressing rooms, men's and women's. Jesus, thinks Herbie as he makes his way down the dingy hallway, why would anybody want to work in the theater after the age of twenty-five? He knocks on the men's dressing room door and the actor playing Telegin opens it. He's in his boxer shorts and a T-shirt. Herbie shakes his hand.

"Hi, I'm Herb Aaron. That was wonderful—really great work. All of you—fantastic show."

"Herbie?" says Bob, who is taking off his makeup at his mirror. "You came *tonight*?" And out comes the laugh again. The other actors cringe and hurry to get dressed and out of there as soon as possible.

Herbie makes a special point of going over to Alvin McConnell, who plays Astrov. He tells him how much he liked his work—especially a scene in Act Two when Astrov is drunk and ranting. Alvin's face lights up—he knows that scene was good and Herbie knows he knows it. They talk a little about people they know in common and promise to get together in New York sometime. Then Herbie sits down in the empty chair next to Bob's corner spot. Bob looks at him like a kid who just scored the winning goal in a soccer game, his eyes lit up with the anticipation of praise. Herbie puts his hand on Bob's head and musses what hair there is left on it.

"I was good, huh?"

"You were great. Best Vanya I've ever seen. Hands down."

"It's going to get better, you know. Why'd you come the first night?"

Herbie just shrugs.

"Are we going out for a drink?"

"If you want."

"Like we used to, remember? After the show? And you would tell me what kind of drink I should have, remember?"

"I remember."

"With Annie."

"Yep."

"What kind of drink should I have tonight?"

"Tonight you should have a hot toddy—good for your throat."

"A hot what?"

"A hot toddy. It's a . . ."

"A hot toddy!" And the horrible laughter again. "Will it make me drunk?"

"Probably."

"You really liked it, huh? I was pretty good."

"You were fucking amazing."

"Yeah, I was."

"All right, get dressed. I'll be in the hall."

"You're going to see Olive."

"Yeah."

"She was good, too."

"She was very good."

"I kept noticing that when I was onstage with her nobody was looking at me."

Herbie smiles and nods.

"Yeah, I know. I'll have to kill her!" And then the shrieking laugh, which propels Herbie out the door and down the hall to the women's dressing room. When he knocks his hand is shaking.

"We're all naked. Come on in!" yells one of the women and they all laugh. There's no relief in the world like the relief of getting through the first audience and having it go well. The ladies' mood is festive.

"Is Olive decent?" he calls through the door.

There's a pause.

"Herbie?"

In a moment the door springs open. Olive has thrown a red silk robe around her shoulders that doesn't begin to cover the fact that she's in her bra and panties.

"Oh, it's *Herbie*," says the actress playing Vanya's mother. "The famous Herbie." And all the girls call out his name like kids in a playground. Olive and Herbie just look at each other.

"I've been telling them a lot about you."

"You're sensational."

Tears spring from her eyes. "You think?"

He nods.

She throws her arms around him and he could turn it into a hug, but he holds back. He's breathless with how good she feels and smells.

"I knew you'd be here."

"Wouldn't have missed it."

"There was a lot of new stuff. Today's rehearsal turned me around completely. It all got deeper and darker. I had no idea what would come out of my mouth tonight."

"She's dark and moody and like . . . shimmering—all at the same time. She's a dazzler. We never had to wonder why all the guys fall in love with her."

She falls back into the hug. "Oh God, I'm glad you're here."

"Me, too."

"I think everybody's going for a drink; you okay with that?"

"Sure. Bob wants to come, too."

"Bob's going out for a drink? That's a first."

"He thinks he can only drink with me. That's the way his mind works. He's got all these little compartments in there and they've all got their own rules. I'll wait for you out here."

At the bar—which is indeed the one Herbie identified on his walk—the acting company is in good spirits. They've commandeered a few tables in the back and put them together to make a party. The booze is flowing, the mood is high, and Herbie is the center of attention. He's a magnet because he's the first outside person to see the play and everyone wants to hear what he has to say. He changes seats often, moving around the table to speak to each of the actors privately, so that they each get the feeling he's really seen their work and appreciates it on a professional level. He knows this game and plays it well.

Alice Tipton, who plays the old nurse, can't get enough of his attention. Whenever he changes seats, she's right behind him. They knew each other years ago when they were both on the voice-over circuit, before Herbie got hot and went on to TV and films. She's actually younger than he is but she's often cast in old-lady roles. She's also one of those actresses of a certain age who still considers herself in the game, as it were, and the more she drinks, the sexier she thinks she is. Her blouse is low cut and she's giving Herbie house seats for the show. He's an appreciative audience and flirts back at her with just enough energy to let her know that it's all in fun. He plays this game well, too.

Bob has managed to get through half of his hot toddy and he's drunk as a skunk. He's slurring his words and putting his face right up next to people and shouting at them. Herbie sits down next to him and puts his arm around him.

"Bobby, can I talk to you?"

"Look at us, Herbie," he says in a loud voice. "We're a family! Isn't it beautiful?" The other actors trade glances. "Wait until the critics get here. They'll carve us up and then we'll be like a real family—we'll want to kill one another!" The laugh is even more detestable when he's drunk.

"Can I talk to you for a second?"

He puts his face right up to Herbie's and whispers. "What is it, Herbie?"

"I'm a little worried about you. I think you got yourself drunk."

"Drunk? Well, maybe a little. What are you worried about?"

"You're going to have a bad headache in the middle of the night and then you're not going to be able to get back to sleep and you have two shows tomorrow."

"Two shows? Oh shit, I have two shows. I'm fucked."

Herbie asks around the table if anybody has any aspirin and one of the girls has Motrin.

"That'll do," says Herbie and he helps Bob get a couple tablets down with a glass of water.

"Where do you live, Bobby? I'm going to take you home."

"No, I'm fine. I can get myself home. I'm not a baby."

"C'mon, get your coat on. I need some fresh air anyway."

He tells Olive he'll be right back and she tells him he's sweet to do this.

"I'm performing a public service."

And as if on cue Bob shouts, "I'm drunk!" and he brays out the laugh again. The cast stands and applauds as Bob and Herbie stumble out of the bar.

Bob is staying in an apartment about six blocks away from the bar. They take their time, walking arm in arm like the old guys do in Italy when they take their after-dinner *passeggiata*. Bob is winding down. His performance adrenaline ran dry an hour ago and the booze hit him like a truck. Herbie almost has to carry him. He ain't heavy, thinks Herbie, he's my brother. Bob links him back to Annie and that time all those years ago. He was around before Candy was born. Bob sticks—like a fishhook.

Bob stops walking.

"Are you going to have sex tonight with Olive?"

"I don't know."

"You really like that stuff."

"I do."

"I guess I should do it, huh?"

Herbie shrugs and they walk for a while, each with his own picture. Then Bob pulls up again.

"I have found it difficult over the years to find a partner for it."

"Pretty basic."

"Problematic for me."

They stand there, feeling the cold.

"Are you going to marry Olive?"

"No, I'm not."

"Why? She's crazy about you."

Herbie looks at him for a moment, waiting for Bob's eyes to focus.

"I'm married, Bobby."

CHAPTER TWENTY-ONE

W HEN HERBIE FINALLY GETS BACK TO THE BAR, THE party's pretty much over. Sam is still there, feeling no pain. He pulls his chair up next to Olive as Herbie takes his coat off and sits to the other side.

"So, you chaps really met at a bar?"

Olive shuffles her chair close to Herbie's and puts her arm through his. "You got a problem with that?"

Sam shakes his head. He's got the picture. Finally. "Don't keep her out too late. Two shows tomorrow." They watch him tipsily make his way out of the bar.

"Nice-looking fella," says Herbie.

"Not my type."

"No?"

"No, I like 'em old and fat."

She holds his eyes. Herbie thinks that he could spend a lot of time with this woman. She moves her chair back around the table so that she can look straight at him.

"You're not drinking tonight," she says.

"You keeping score?"

"I'm a bartender."

They smile.

"Okay," she says, "tell me what you really thought."

"Of you?"

She nods and takes a deep breath.

"I told you."

"Now really."

He tries not to fall into her eyes, which are dark and serious. "Okay. You have unbelievable presence—like star presence. We can't take our eyes off you."

"You or everybody?"

"I actually took a moment to check out other people's faces. It's not just me. Second, you're an actor, without a doubt. You're at home up there; you stand on the stage, in the light, being watched by the rest of us sitting in the dark and you love it. That's an actor. The rest is tricks."

"How was the rest?"

He shrugs. "I just tell you what I thought?"

She nods.

"Okay, there were two moments—exactly two—where your acting wasn't good."

He sees her stiffen. "Where?"

"You know exactly where. Both times you were showing us what you were feeling instead of feeling it. And they stood out—because, in general, you weren't doing that."

"In the first scene," she says.

"Yep. First entrance."

"But that's her showing, not me. That's Yelena doing bad acting."

"Yeah, I'd be real careful with that shit. Especially on your first entrance."

She files that. "Where else? Oh, I know where."

He nods. "So, enough said. Other than those two it was exquisite; it was seamless. I was never looking at you—only her. Really beautiful acting."

He watches her face flush with pride because she knows he's

saying the truth. Why, he thinks, is her face so fascinating tonight? Maybe it's that now he knows her as an actor and he can see more of her, deeper levels, more interesting angles.

"So what's the story, mister? You gonna make a play for me or not?"

Nothing changes on Herbie's face; inside is chaos.

"I made my play the first moment I saw you, remember? But that doesn't mean we're going to do anything about it."

"Physically, you mean." Her serious face is a tease.

"Yeah. It might be a good idea just to keep things the way they are."

"Annie told me you would say that."

He stares at her.

"But she also told me that if you did say it, you'd be lying."

"Really." He's not comfortable with this.

"She's here, Herbie," she says, leaning forward across the table. "She always will be. A person that huge doesn't just go away."

He knows this.

"And I thought you liked being with two women."

If he knew how to blush, he would.

"Tell me about the luftmensch."

"She told you about that?"

"Only that it was one of your past lives. She said you would tell me."

"Oh, she did."

Olive nods.

"If you believe in that shit. Annie always wanted to try everything, so once she heard about this past-life therapist, she had to sign us right up."

"I looked it up. A luftmensch is like a dreamer, right? A Jewish dreamer."

"The weird thing is that I don't think I had ever heard the word before it popped out of my mouth in that session. I mean, maybe I did—subconsciously in some book or magazine somewhere—but I have absolutely no memory of ever having heard that expression—and the moment I was going into the past life—you know, the woman was giving me the spiel about 'tell me what you see'—all that crap—and it just popped right out of my mouth. I'm a luftmensch, I said. She had no idea what I was talking about."

"It's Yiddish, right?"

"Yeah. It means 'air-man.' Like a guy who—if he didn't have heavy shoes on, would just float up and away over the rooftops. The image in my mind was that rabbinical-looking guy in the Chagall painting, floating over the house at a funny angle—like the Tower of Pisa."

"So what did this luftmensch do—in your past life? Did he have a job or did he just float?"

"No, that was the whole point. He was a teacher—a sort of rabbinical type. He had a school in a beautiful place in the country with green rolling hills and a lake. A school for young women."

"Ah."

"Well, they weren't all young. They were all different ages, I think. This was a lot of lifetimes ago so I can't remember exactly, but many of them were young. I do remember that. I can picture the young ones."

"And you taught them . . . ?"

"I taught them how to discover all the pleasure that was available to them in their bodies."

"Ah."

"They wore these long robes; all white; made of a light material that you could kind of see through. And no one wore any underwear of any kind. That was a rule."

"Uh-huh. And what did the luftmensch wear?"

"Also like a caftan, made of a darker material—a rich woven fabric of many colors.

"Biblical."

"Yes, it was."

"Underwear?"

"No. No underwear at this school."

"And you fucked them all."

"Well there, you see? Everybody goes there—right to the fucking. But I have to tell you—as a man who has spent many lifetimes in the study of such things—fucking is not always the best way to bring a woman to the highest, most ecstatic states. Nothing against it, mind you. It's a wonderful thing; makes the world go 'round and all that, but not necessarily the best mode of transportation when you're going up the ladder to paradise. In fact, fucking is best used as a way to bring a woman back down to earth, as it were, because you can't live your daily life in a state of extended ecstasy—you wouldn't get anything done. You can't drive, for example, when you're in that state; you can't shop or anything, go to the hardware store . . ."

"I never thought of it that way."

"Well," he shrugs, "now you can."

"So the luftmensch wouldn't get around to fucking them until the end of the session?"

"Yes, often at the end. Or occasionally in the middle. Or every now and then at the beginning, depending on the particular lesson he was teaching that day. I mean he could be teaching the one about knocking off a quickie, in which case . . ." He shrugs.

"Right. So this wasn't tiring for you? I mean how many students did you have at any given time?"

"Oh, quite a few—maybe a dozen, but they wouldn't, you

know, work every day. We'd sit in a circle and the others would watch as each girl had her personal experience."

"Ah, so they'd all watch you."

"Well, there are many ways to learn, you know. Many different avenues through which the information can enter you, so to speak."

She looks at him in disbelief and shakes her head. "Herbie, this wasn't a past life. This is you. Now."

"No, no, this was long, long ago in a galaxy far away. You could tell by the costumes."

"Remind me in the years to come—just in case I forget—what a grand and wonderful bullshitter you are. Unbelievable."

Herbie doesn't deny it. He watches the color come up in her cheeks and her eyes sizzle like the ocean when the sun falls into it. Pretty good foreplay, he thinks, for a geezer. At this moment he knows exactly how she'd like to be touched and where and at what speed. And he knows exactly what her response will be. God, he thinks, if I had instincts like this for acting I would have been Marlon fucking Brando.

"But it's not just the sex," he says. "There's another side to the luftmensch."

"To you, you mean. There's another side to you."

He shrugs.

"Tell me about the other side."

Herbie puts his elbows on the table and folds his hands in front of his mouth as if to stop himself from speaking. His face is the face of an old rabbi; he's quiet for a long time.

"There's the alone side," he says finally.

Olive waits him out.

"He lives inside his head, this guy; he's a muser, a philosopher, a solitary soul. He likes to tumble his thoughts over and around, catching glances of them in every different light. A hundred years ago, in the shtetls, these guys were always there. The air men. They never worked a day in their life; they never lifted a finger. Occasionally they hung out with other bums like themselves and philosophized about angels on the heads of pins. Occasionally, out of pity, people would bring them a sandwich or something—so they wouldn't starve to death."

Olive waits.

"There are these two sides to him."

"To you. Two sides to you."

He says nothing.

"I know that you talk to yourself."

He just stares at her.

"Annie told me. And I saw you doing it one time when you came to the bar. You were going on and on about something, cracking yourself up."

"Jesus Christ."

Olive smiles now. "I'll make you a deal."

"What?"

"Come home with me now and stay with me tonight—and then tomorrow you can talk to yourself all day. I have two shows anyway."

This almost gets a laugh, but he shakes it off.

"I'm gonna get old and sick," he says. "It's not far off. What do you do then?"

She shakes her head and shrugs. "I don't know. I honest-to-God can't give you an answer about that, Herbie. I mean, you're about to go away, right? To do your movie?"

"Day after tomorrow."

"And I'm here doing the play for another month. By the time we see each other again, we'll be completely different people. Isn't that what you believe?"

He takes a moment to think about that. "So, who knows? That's what you're saying?"

"I know that I want to be with you tonight. I have no doubts about that. You know that nervousness you have when you're about to go to bed with someone new? I don't have it. You'll just be you and I'll just be me and we'll be fine, whatever happens. Or doesn't happen. We can't miss, Herbie."

She's just hit him with his own philosophy. What's he going to do, argue?

"I play a game with myself sometimes," he says. "I'm walking up to the deli on Broadway to get milk for my coffee or something and I say, all right, either I could walk down West End Avenue to Eighty-second Street, make a left and go up to Broadway, or I could walk a block farther on West End and go up Eighty-first Street. And I say, easy Herb; take a moment; this decision could change everything. Say I take Eighty-second Street and I run into a guy I haven't seen in years and he says what a coincidence! I'm casting a play Off-Broadway and you're perfect for the lead—I didn't know you were back in New York. And I do the play and it's a big hit and I get a movie out of it that gets me an Oscar nomination and my whole career takes off again. Or maybe I take Eighty-first Street and I step off the curb in the middle of the block and a Chinese food delivery guy coming the wrong way runs into me with his bike and they rush me to the hospital where I get one of those infections that eats your skin and they have no cure for and I lie there in pain for the rest of my miserable life. You know?"

She nods. She knows. "So?" she says.

"So what?"

She opens her arms to him. "So take Eighty-second Street."

He wants to enter the embrace she offers; he wants to smell her hair and feel her warmth.

"There are things," he says, shaking his head.

"Like what?"

"Like I have this cream. I have to put it on my ass sometimes when I get an itch down there."

She stares at him in disbelief. He raises his eyebrows in innocence and holds his hands out in the surrender position—as if to say, hey, I thought this was a good time to get everything out onto the table. Then he sighs and looks around for the waiter, who must have given up and gone home. Olive starts to get her coat on and he thinks, so where are we going? My hotel? Her apartment? She'll probably want to have her own toothbrush. He nods to himself. Girls don't want to mess with somebody else's toothbrush. He gives up on the waiter and walks toward the bar to pay the check.

"Hit the ball, Herb," he says out loud. "Just waltz right up to the fucking ball and whack away."

ACKNOWLEDGMENTS

I WOULD LIKE TO THANK A NUMBER OF PEOPLE WHOSE advice and encouragement helped me while I was writing this book: my fiercely loyal agents, Jane Dystel and Miriam Goderich; everyone at Overlook Press, especially my editor, Stephanie Gorton, and, of course, the estimable Peter Mayer. And, in no particular order: Jane Kramer, Stephen Bochco, Jim Moore, JoAnn Verburg, Susan Liederman, David Liederman, Ron Shechtman, Lynne Meadow, Jeffrey Sweet, Bruce Adgate, Joanna Ross, Jeffrey Isaac, Sophie Clarke, John Pankow, Kristine Pankow, Martin Steubenrauch, Karen Bamonte, Carol Venezia, Michael Venezia, Pam Moskow, Ron McLarty, David Rapkin . . . and anyone I may have forgotten.

ML

3/12